A BATCH OF TWENTY

CHRIS EDWARDS

ISBN: 9781777776152

Edited by: Stephanie Fysh

Cover design by: Cindy Rose

PART ONE

1

PALE LIGHT BROKE the dark. A man held his flashlight beside his face; circling around bins and machinery, toward the center of the ship's hold, listening for a response.

"Smart cargo, c'mon! Hands up if you got 'em."

Two Load Bearers slowly raised their arms. The man nodded, sweeping his light past the massive robots, illuminating the iron walls of the hold: the displays still blinking, the ship powering down from its trip across the water.

There were 40 vats of seed and produce and freeze-dried meat in this hold, flat-surfaced, square-cornered, stacked in an uneven row that got as high as two stories. They were the sort of thing the Island needed most, although someday, the man hoped, it would not. He had a little garden, next to his flat in the Village, filled with veggies invigorated by sea air.

It was due to these thoughts, perhaps, that the man passed his light twice over Ethelred before noticing him, seated in a small pocket of space between two of the seed vats, his hand raised just above his head. The Helper said nothing as the light shone over him, and then away, and then over him again. He merely waited. He had raised his hand, as requested, and that was enough.

3

The light fell on him a third time and stayed there. Ethelred heard the man approach. The light redirected and the man stood face to face with him. The man was a tall man.

"Name?"

"Ethelred."

"Third Anglo-Saxon king since yesterday," the man said quietly. "*Integrated Foods* sent you back?"

Ethelred pointed to his foot. "I have a broken ankle."

The man dipped his flashlight, beaming it on the cast. "And *I-F* sent you 200 miles off coast instead of just keeping you in Virginia Beach and patching you up there?"

"Yes."

The man chewed his lip a moment. He swept his light in a high arc around the hold.

"Funny stuff going on around here lately," he said. "Real funny stuff."

2

ETHELRED WAS UNABLE to walk, so he waited in the hold until the first of the Load Bearers had stacked within its gullet both of the seed vats that flanked him. He then rode the robot's arm up to the top of those vats and took a seat. Cargo transported cargo out of the ship's hold and into *Amino Corp.'s* factory docking bay.

Amino was a small manufacturer, its two factory complexes having expanded out from the remnants of a long-defunct oil drilling platform in the Atlantic. The platform sat on a latitudinal point level with the old state border between Virginia and Maryland— now a national border between Union East and Sothentide. *Amino* produced tech products, mostly: AI-equipped diagnostic equipment and sensor suites, nanotech surgical swarms (sold by the canister), and construction and military drones. And, of course, one product that was not a machine.

The Helpers.

Ethelred sat evenly on the vats—the Load Bearer pressing on, like some weary dinosaur, toward the far end of the bay. The cargo ship that had brought them remained in the dock, its snub nose tilted upward, while robots in a myriad of shapes and sizes—donuts, spheres, platforms—any configuration save humanoid—busied themselves emptying and refilling it. The Load Bearer was designed to bear great cargo too, and not just of a volume measurable in units of length and weight—it could also bear information, in enormous amounts, encrypted to the highest levels.

They passed a cart carrying six Helpers. The Helpers sat in two rows, facing ahead: their bodies human, implicitly male; their flesh chalk white; their expressions alert but indifferent. Ethelred watched the tops of their heads glide by, the cart continuing a little way past them before climbing a ramp and disappearing into the mouth of the cargo ship, bound for Sothentide.

At the center of the far wall was a large opening leading to a collection of tunnels, through which goods were transported from the docking bay into the factory proper and outside. Here the number of little robots became so thick that the Load Bearer was forced to stop and wait for an opportunity to take a step—and it was during this pause that Ethelred saw a man approaching them, frantically waving his arms, bidding them to stay where they were.

3

ETHELRED AND THE MAN swept quietly through Tunnel Seven in a self-driving cart. The man sat uncomfortably in his seat, like he wanted to slouch but was too agitated to do it properly. He was young.

"Have you sustained further damage?" he asked, flicking a finger toward Ethelred's cast. He looked around, but the tunnel had little to see.

"No. The Load Bearer transported me the entire way."

"That wasn't supposed to happen. That was a miscommunication." The man tapped his knee. "Keep it to yourself."

They rode another minute or so in silence, the tunnel rising gradually, its running lights blurring as the cart picked up speed. The man checked his mobile, batting aside holographic displays with some irritation. Ethelred noted that the displays were camouflaged from his side—glossy and opaque. This was a security feature most users didn't bother with anymore.

"You're from Sothentide," the Helper said, finally. His companion jumped.

"How do you know that?"

"Adam Balendran. You grew up in Charleston."

The man closed his display. "How do you know that?"

"I'm able to view public-facing staff lists for *Amino*. Anyone can. You were a student in USC's Faculty of Artificial Organism Development, correct? You are a cognitive programming theorist, junior grade. Am I somehow of interest to a cognitive programming theorist?"

"I'm just supposed to fetch you."

"I have a broken ankle—it's a technician I need."

"I expect we'll see to that too."

"Are we not headed to a repair bay now?" Ethelred looked around, the tunnel growing dimmer.

"No. We're headed to a research facility here in Old Factory. They're sequestering you for a little while. They need your help, Ethelred."

"Who does?"

"My superiors."

"Regarding marketing for food and drink?"

"No, Ethelred." Adam managed a small smile. "Regarding the future of this company."

4

ADAM TOLD THE cart to stop before an unmarked doorway. Helped the Helper dismount. Then he departed—leaving Ethelred standing on one leg inside a room, holding a beam of the low ceiling overhead to keep his balance.

Before him were 19 other Helpers, all seated on benches placed around the room, motionless and silent. This is a storage locker, Ethelred thought. He took a step forward, nearly collapsing before catching another beam and steadying himself. He balanced on his right leg and hopped gingerly toward the bench. None of the Helpers rose to assist him. None even turned to look.

Ethelred pivoted on his right heel and landed hard on the edge of a bench.

Next to him was a Helper who resembled him almost exactly, except this one was missing his right hand. He was small, with straight black hair and a pallor like bleached bone. His eyes were large and outlined in black, as though tattooed that way, and likewise his lips and nostrils. The Helper's left hand had long, thin fingers of almost equal length, which he'd placed calmly over the bandaged stump. His posture suggested conscious effort, as though being seated were not something he could forget about once he'd sat down.

Ethelred turned to the one-handed Helper. "I'm Ethelred, property of *Integrated Foods,* Virginia Beach, Virginia," he said.

The Helper turned to him. "I'm Egbert, property of *Peachy Corp.,* Mobile, Alabama," he replied. There was no need to say more than the state, because Helpers were legal only in Sothentide.

There was no need to say anything more at all.

After a while the door opened and two large men entered the room. Each took Ethelred by one arm and helped him onto another cart, waiting outside in the tunnel.

5

THE NEXT ROOM was small and bright. In the center was an empty stool, before a curved table seating Adam, an older man of about 40, and a young woman. Adam's space was cluttered with an open mobile display, a full mug of coffee, and a pink pastry box. The other two had kept their spaces clean.

The woman sat in the middle. She looked up at Ethelred, still standing in the doorway, and motioned him to enter. Ethelred again hopped his way to a seat, while the woman waited, watching him.

"My name is Nan Fulton," she said. "I'm Lead Researcher, Unit Four, Helper Division." She waved a hand at her colleagues on either side. "Adam you've already met. He serves as my assistant on this project. And this is Bob Barnum, our AI psychoanalyst, senior grade."

Bob nodded curtly. "We've brought you here to answer a few questions, Ethelred," he said. "Do you have any of your own, before we begin?"

Ethelred did. "I was told that I'd be shipped to Amino Island for the purpose of repairing my broken ankle," he said. He addressed only Nan Fulton, for he was aware of her reputation. "Does this questioning in some way involve my ankle?"

Bob glanced at Nan. "Not directly, no," he said.

"The Helpers we've been questioning over the last two days are all damaged in some way. They were all made here, in this building, obviously, and they've been brought back for a free repair. And it's my understanding—" again Bob looked to Nan before continuing— "that those repairs will take place."

After a pause, during which Nan and Ethelred sat looking at one another, the researchers began their questioning.

"You're one of a fleet of 10 owned by *Integrated Foods,* correct?" Nan asked.

"Correct."

"Your company purchased you to help predict rises and dips in popularity of food products and then propose new products to best match those trends," she went on, blandly. "In less than two years, you have proposed more than 400 new food product ideas, 44 of which were approved by the company's marketing department. All 44 have proven profitable. Am I correct and up to date?"

"Yes."

"You can taste things as well as a human can, right? That's listed here as a customization."

"Yes. Certainly better than any other Helpers I've met."

Nan raised an eyebrow. Bob nudged her and broke in.

"Does that matter to you, Ethelred?" he asked. "Being better than the others?"

"I mention it because it's noteworthy."

"Does it make *you* noteworthy?"

"Only if *I-F*'s aware of it."

Bob began tapping something on his display. Nan resumed. "What is your goal, in your work? What do you wish to achieve?"

"An appropriate level of function."

"Don't you function appropriately now?"

"No."

"Why not?"

"My mobility is compromised."

Nan nodded. "What about before you were damaged? Didn't you function adequately to complete your tasks?"

"Yes."

"Isn't that an 'appropriate level of function'?"

"Functioning adequately to complete my tasks is not appropriate for *me,* Dr. Fulton."

Bob broke in: "Why not?"

"My cost is considerable," Ethelred said, "such that I am one of only 10 of my kind to be purchased by *Integrated Foods*. It would not be in keeping with the value placed upon me to perform merely 'adequately.'"

Bob and Nan looked thoughtful. Adam tore off a piece of French cruller and sucked it into his mouth.

"What's 'adequate' function, to you?" Nan asked.

"To perform only to the benchmarks set out for me by human beings. My purchasers at *Integrated Foods*."

Bob opened his mouth and then Nan held up one finger and he shut it again.

"So am I correct in assuming, Ethelred," she said, leaning in and resting her chin on both fists, "that being put to the use which your purchasers intend for you—I mean, that's the whole reason they're your purchasers, isn't it—counts merely as adequate function? A performance unworthy of a Helper such as yourself?"

"You are correct, Dr. Fulton."

"But this isn't a view shared by the other Helpers in your fleet."

"No. I exceed adequacy by a margin quantifiably higher than the others."

She returned to her notes. "Your injury: it's self-inflicted."

"It is not."

"It's a result of a choice you made, isn't it?"

"I stepped one foot into the vat of an industrial mixer. One of the blades struck me on the foot, twisting it almost completely around. But it wasn't as though I wished to do it."

"You didn't intend to do it."

"Yes, I intended it." Ethelred wondered how she could be so dense. "But it wasn't something I would have done if there'd been another option. One of my colleagues was falling into the mixer. I happened to be within reach, and so I moved forward. The angle of our bodies around the edge was such that I had to put one foot in the vat."

"This colleague, as you put it, was another Helper. You saved his life."

"Yes."

"And contaminated a large volume of tapioca pudding in the process."

Ethelred was a little surprised. "He would have been killed, Dr. Fulton. Even if he hadn't been, his fall would have contaminated the vat anyway. Are you suggesting I should have let him die?"

Bob interjected. "You said, 'I happened to be within reach, and so I moved forward.' We have the incident report. There was someone else within reach too, Ethelred: a human employee. Shouldn't you have relied on that individual to save the Helper?"

"No."

"Why not?"

"Because she might have failed. Whereas I would not have failed."

"But for your intervention, the Helper would have died. It is unlikely your human co-worker could have saved him. Correct?"

"Correct."

"It sounds like you consider yourself more valuable than the humans you work with," Nan said.

"Not at all. A human's value is qualitative; mine is quantitative. It's a different thing."

"What is your value, Ethelred?"

"My unit cost was $2.2 million at purchase, less a five percent volume discount, since the entire fleet was purchased at once. I am, based on my work, directly responsible for an average increase in *I-F*'s total value of two percent—the others in our fleet accounting, on average, for 0.4 percent each. Obviously, our fleet has been hugely successful for *I-F,* allowing it to take leadership of the bulk food market in Sothentide, Union East and the Center States."

"And based on that," Nan went on, "what do you calculate to be the cost to *Integrated Foods* of your absence?"

"That is best measured per annum, Dr. Fulton. My projection would be a loss in future growth of one percent per year, going forward—assuming, somehow, that I am unable to return."

"You don't think the others could pick up the slack?"

"There is no reason to think so."

"Right." Nan paused, mulling something over.

During this moment the mood in the room grew suspenseful; it being clear to the Helper, as well as the two men, that no one was to speak until Nan ceded her verbal space. This she did, eventually, to Bob—who seemed, to Ethelred, to be more animated by the proceedings than Nan was.

"How much was that vat worth, Ethelred? The pudding, I mean."

"The mixer is the size of a house, Dr. Barnum. That volume of product would sell, in total, for about $200,000."

"Whereas you're worth—what—four million? I mean, if you combine purchase cost and contributions to annual growth?"

"But I didn't—"

"It's obviously possible," Bob continued, "that more than your foot could've ended up in that vat. So you cost the company $200,000, and risked a far greater loss, simply to save another Helper's life. A Helper that—according to you—could not have replaced you."

Helpers were famous for their lack of extraneous movement—as one Union Eastern writer put it, in terms of body language they were mutes. Yet Ethelred provided for his questioners something they recognized as annoyance. "Doctors, it seems as though I'm being interrogated. At no point following my accident did *I-F* criticize me for costing them money. The decision I made was a split-second one, and I believe, if you ask either the Helper I saved or the human employee present, either will tell you that it was the right thing to do."

"Yes, Ethelred, of course it was," said Bob. "It's just that—we've been interviewing Helpers for almost two days now, and none of them have given answers quite like yours."

Nan turned to Adam. "We need a moment."

Adam stood up, addressing the Helper. "You must return to the waiting area, with the others."

Ethelred began to rise, awkwardly as ever. Nan shook her head.

"Wait," she said. "Sit." She turned to Bob. "He can't walk properly. He can stay here." And then to Adam: "Put up a dampening field." She repeated it, because Adam had not heard her.

Ethelred watched the assistant push his pastry box and cup of coffee to one side and pull up a shallow holo-display, tapping a couple of icons. Now Ethelred's vision began to distort—as though someone had poured clear syrup over his eyes. The three humans and their desktop warped and wobbled; it became impossible for Ethelred to see more than movement and color. His hearing became muffled too—crisp sounds going fuzzy, thickening; growing indistinct; until he could be sure of nothing but tones.

Their discussion went on for some time. Ethelred saw Nan's outline shift suddenly toward Adam, heard the pitch of her voice rise sharply, angrily; then the shape receded. He heard Bob's voice, then Nan's again, sounding conversational.

Ethelred was worried. He knew that if his repair had been promised to him, he had no reason to believe it would not happen, and yet the circumstances that had brought him here appeared fraudulent. The scientists claimed to have been questioning Helpers for days now—had Egbert been here that long, still unrepaired? Was *Integrated*

Foods to be without his services for some time? If so, was *Integrated Foods* aware of that?

He saw the shapes of Adam's head and shoulders collapse into a blob. There was movement in the mushy pink visual in front of him, and then Ethelred smelled the sharp odor of Pumpkin Spice, almost certainly part of a danish. The dampening field seemed to have no effect on Ethelred's sense of smell, which was particularly acute.

Ethelred knew much about this flavor—this Pumpkin Spice. It was, depending on where you lived, either a wistful evocation of fall or a derisive stand-in for commercialism. There were more than 70 methods of producing it. Nor was it simply a flavor. Studies had proven that a piece of cloth of a certain color would be described as "Pumpkin Spice" by a significant minority of any population, and that a significant minority of that minority would describe the cloth as "pungent" or "tasty." The Helper's mind, focused as it was, had made it easy for him to plot the flavor's dips and rises in esteem over the years and to propose various alternatives for *Integrated Foods*'s fall offerings; these had included a carbonated pink lemonade that consumers, remarkably, seemed to associate with nothing at all, save its being completely unlike Pumpkin Spice. Ethelred had called the drink Passive Aggression. It sold like wildfire.

Around him the scene began to clear. The three questioners returned to focus, all of them facing the Helper. In front of Adam, on a plate, sat a half-eaten danish, the filling beneath its latticework pastry tinted dark orange.

6

SHORTLY AFTERWARD ETHELRED was returned to the Helpers' room. It was as he'd left it. None of the others had stirred.

He clutched the beams overhead, making the same half-stumble half-simian swing to maneuver himself back to the bench. The relief was instant: at once his mind ceased calculating how long the ankle would hold, how much further damage he might take, how compromised he would continue to be till it was fixed.

Somewhere in this building—maybe on this floor—Ethelred had been created. His brain had been coded with all relevant information about Pumpkin Spice and thousands of other flavors before he'd first opened his eyes. The body he'd had then was the one he had now: he'd taken his first steps without hesitation, recognized and named every taste and smell the first time he sensed them. To be a Helper was to begin life as a mature being, made to order. Individuality, so far as it mattered, was a product of one's body of work.

And no one had a body of work like Ethelred's.

Yet here he sat, one of 20. All of them in some way injured: lacerations, a patched eye, dislocated joints; problems with equilibrium. In the far corner sat an old one: maybe 13 years old, with wrinkled skin and a shattered knee. Beside him was a Helper whose chest and neck were bandaged heavily.

Ethelred's mind continued its threshing, till he heard a sharp cry. The bandaged Helper was buckling: his head, which up till now had sat above a massing of foam and gauze around his neck, slumped downward, his nose now resting in the foam, eyes mostly shut.

The others listened to his breathing, muffled by the foam.

"How many days have you been here?" Ethelred asked Egbert, as if to change the subject.

"Two days. Eight Helpers arrived after I did, including you."

"Have you been interviewed?"

"Each of us has left this room once, for about an hour, to be questioned by *Amino* cognitive programmers."

"And what did they question you about?" Ethelred wished he sounded less interested.

"They asked me about my job. What I thought it was."

"How did you answer them?"

"I told them my job was me."

7

AT SEVEN O'CLOCK the next morning, 20 trays of food were delivered to the Helpers' room. Each tray was partitioned into fifths, the fare ranging from brown to gray; in consistency from pudding to hardtack. The Helpers sat in silence, chewing and swallowing the same breakfast they'd been eating their whole lives. Thinking nothing of it.

Only Ethelred, who could taste things as a human could, felt differently. But he'd learned that if he thought of this not as eating but as absorbing, like a machine absorbs energy, then it became more bearable. It was during this process of visualization—Ethelred imagining himself an old-time train boiler, taking shovelfuls of coal into his fiery maw—that the guards entered the Helpers' room. They apologized for interrupting mealtime, and took Ethelred away.

***

The interview room was unchanged, Ethelred sitting before the three scientists. Adam had swapped out his danish for a pair of frosted donuts. Nan looked overtired.

"So you were worth 2.2 mil," she said, as though the last interview had never ended.

"That was my unit cost, if you ignore the volume discount. But factoring in Sothentide's currency decline, my current value would be 2.8."

Nan closed her eyes. "And two years from now?"

"If tensions with Union East remain high? Nearly four."

"So, diplomacy being what it is on the continent, Helpers only get more valuable."

"So it seems."

Nan swept a hand through something on her mobile display. "What about obsolescence?"

"I am not obsolete."

"In a few years' time you might be."

"In a few years' time I'll be dead. My kind will not be obsolete." Ethelred tugged on his right pant leg, causing his leg to straighten then return to position. "There have been no significant innovations in *Amino*'s Helper design schema for more than a decade. It's unlikely the company will develop and market a model that can outperform me anytime soon."

Bob spoke next. "Do you think innovations have to be 'significant,' Ethelred? What about small changes? Slight improvements to synaptic speed, refinement of the senses?"

"None of those changes would justify the cost of designing, much less purchasing an entirely new Helper," Ethelred said. "Our base cost is too high."

"What about improved mimicry of the human form?"

That's the oddest question yet, Ethelred thought. He considered the best way to answer it, noticing that all three scientists were holding their breaths, waiting for him. So he let them wait, just long enough to cause discomfort.

"What benefit would that provide me?" he asked, finally.

"Are you asking us," Bob replied, "or yourself?"

"I'm asking you."

"You have no opinion of your own?"

The Helper's eyes darted from one scientist to the next. "I favor only those upgrades which my purchasers at *Integrated Foods* deem necessary for me to perform my function."

"But you told us—" Bob sat back in his chair, lacing his fingers together—"that to perform only to the level your purchaser expects is to perform at a level beneath what is justified by your purchase cost."

"Yes."

"So it seems to me—to us—" Bob looked quickly to his team lead— "that you ought to have an opinion."

"I have no opinion. I favor only those upgrades which my purchasers at *Integrated Foods* deem necessary for me to perform my function," the Helper repeated.

"Oh stop it!" Nan said. "We're asking you a direct question. You're capable of answering it, and yet you won't. I *command you* to do so. Would you favor improved mimicry of the human form? If the choice was yours, Ethelred."

"I favor only those upgrades which my purchasers at *Integrated Foods* deem necessary for me to perform my function."

"Why?"

"Because without my purchaser, I have no purpose. No reason to exist at all."

Nan seethed. She ordered Adam to bring up the dampening field. He did not respond, so she turned and cuffed him on the side of the head. Adam jumped; brought up the display screen as requested, began tapping icons. In so doing he struck his coffee mug, sloshing cold liquid on his team leader's lap.

Nan stood up: pinched her slacks above the knee, wicking away the moisture. "Unfocused and lazy. Unfocused and lazy . . . "

She returned to her seat.

"It's the same thing—the same dodge," Bob said. "All these damaged Helpers have shown signs of a humane sensibility, through their willingness to risk their lives for another. Implicit in that act is the belief that their own worth is not purely quantitative, despite what they say to us. But when we start moving them toward the idea of their own humanity, they start sounding like robots. How can it be both?"

"I want to figure this out," Nan said, "but we can't tell him too much. So . . . how?" She leaned back, rubbing her eyes. She felt like shit. She was glad the dampening field was up—if nothing else, it allowed her to relax for a moment, hidden from the Helper's eyes and ears.

But Ethelred could see, and hear, her perfectly.

8

THE HELPER OBSERVED his three human interlocutors, each sunk in the postures that defined them: Nan, frustration; Bob, fascination; Adam, humiliation. Whatever button the junior assistant was supposed to press, he hadn't.

"This one can make the leap," Bob said. "He's considered the value of a Helper's life more deeply than the others. He defended his act of self-sacrifice almost to the point of anger."

"Self-sacrifice, on its own, isn't enough."

"It's a human value, Nan."

"It's a mammalian trait! Martin needs more than that." Nan tapped her finger on the desk. "They have to declare it. On tape, and without being prompted. 'I am a human being.' Declare yourself human and you have human rights." She looked at the Helper and frowned. "Self-sacrifice is a step in the right direction, but as long as he's defining himself in terms of 'unit cost' and 'value to the company' or whatever, there's no argument a lawyer can spin out of that."

"If we have, say, another 10 Helpers, maybe another week, we'll get there. I can prepare a request for an extension—"

"But they're all the same, basically—even this one. He's just unusually pompous." Nan sounded defeated. "They don't see themselves the way Martin sees them. They're designed not to. That's what makes them worth buying!"

She waved mockingly at Ethelred, who did not react.

"Helpers don't desire anything more than to meet the intent of their creators. And unlike us, they know exactly who their creators are, and precisely what the intent is."

"This one's exceeding his owner's intent."

"His owner's intent, Bob, is to make the most money possible. Martin may be Division Head, but he can't change that reality."

"There is that second line of inquiry I proposed . . . if you recall?" Bob said. "We've brought them here under false pretenses, and by now they're starting to suspect something's wrong. But every one of them assumes their purchaser has been fooled too. Which only strengthens their loyalty to the purchaser, and their willingness to defer to the purchaser's will."

"Which is a psychoanalytical conclusion on your part, and therefore irrelevant to this exercise," Nan said quietly.

"This is our last test subject. What's the point of keeping it from him? We've kept it from all the others and gotten nowhere. Tell him his company deceived him—after all he's done for them—and it may trigger something."

"You're projecting, aren't you?"

Bob cleared his throat.

"What you propose," Nan went on, "is that a Helper like this can feel betrayal. And I'd argue no— that a Helper *cannot* be betrayed even if he's been lied to. Not even if *Integrated Foods* tells this one that it's sending him here to fix his ankle—while, in the meantime, it's taking a payoff from us, then distributing his tasks to nine lower-performing Helpers in the fleet . . . What are you looking so green about?"

"Nothing," Adam whispered. He pushed his mug away with one finger.

"Anyway, you go ahead," Nan said to Bob. "As you've put it, more or less, we have nothing left to lose. And it's not like any of these Helpers are gonna leave the Island again."

***

Ethelred watched with interest as Adam made a show of switching off the dampening field. He glanced to his left, to Bob's smiling face.

"Just a couple more," Bob said. "Ethelred, how would you feel if I told you that your purchaser hadn't been truthful with you?"

"Dubious."

"You'd be suspicious?"

"Of the claim, yes."

"You don't think it's credible that *Integrated Foods* would mislead you?"

"No. It is impossible." Ethelred stared at Nan and said no more.

"All right then." Nan looked wearily at her two colleagues. "Anything else you'd like to ask him?"

Bob shook his head. After a moment, so did Adam.

"If you're through questioning me," Ethelred said, "may I make a request?"

"Of course." Bob brought up his mobile display and poised a finger next to it. Ethelred turned from Nan to Adam.

"I would like one of those donuts."

9

THE GUARDS RETURNED and escorted Ethelred, donut in hand, out of the room and into the cart.

"You sharing?" one of them asked.

"I'm afraid not," said Ethelred.

His fellow Helpers ignored him as he found his way back to the bench. He placed the donut, a pillowy dainty with a pearlescent top and golden cake, on his lap.

He tapped Egbert on the leg.

"I'll need your help in a moment," he said. "Do you object?"

Egbert shook his head.

"All right. YOU!" Ethelred called across the room, to the slumping Helper with the bandaged neck and nose in the foam. "What is your name?"

The Helper's response was unintelligible.

"Are you all right?" asked Ethelred.

The other Helpers turned and looked at him. Ethelred ignored them, repeating again, "are you all right?" and getting no answer he could make out.

"Perhaps," he started—but the words seemed to grind to a halt. He tried again. "Perhaps one of our colleagues can put your head right." He gestured to the Helpers on either side of the stricken one. And they did help: one leaning over and with his good hand stabilizing the Helper's body, while the other one, with his good arm, lifted the head back up and balanced it so the Helper could lean backward against the wall, rather than forward. The Helper smiled. His face bore none of the evidence of massacre that his neck did.

"Are you all right?" Ethelred asked.

"Yes," the Helper managed.

"Every Helper in here," Ethelred went on, "is damaged in some way. Aren't we?" It surprised the others that he vocalized this, obvious though it was— observations were usually kept in one's head. To the one they'd assisted, he asked again: "What is your name?"

"Alfred."

"How did you get here, Alfred?"

"I work at a zoo, optimizing nutrient protocols for large carnivores. They have tremendous destructive capacity. I saved another Helper from being eaten."

"I saved a Helper from falling into a vat of pudding," said Ethelred. "Did we all save someone? Some other Helper?"

Egbert raised his bandaged stump. "A Helper on my lab floor stumbled while holding a laser-hatchet— he pierced a tank of acid as he fell. I placed my hand on the fissure to prevent it from reaching his face." Now all the other Helpers began speaking at once, each relaying his story: 17 tales of bodily sacrifice made to preserve a fellow Helper's life. The stories, by virtue of their sameness and the sameness of the persons telling them, fell into a kind of harmony, unified by placement of nouns and verbs and common verbal digressions. And they all ended the same way: with the Helper being put on the shelf, awaiting medical care, and being told, unexpectedly, that this care would be provided on Amino Island.

The din ceased. Ethelred asked Egbert if he might allow his good arm to serve as a hook to hold onto, so that Ethelred might stand. This he did, and so Ethelred was able to address his seated audience, holding up the donut.

They stared at him blankly. Some stared at the donut.

"I can taste things," Ethelred said, taking a bite. "Just like the humans can." He turned his wrist slowly from side to side, as though putting the gnawn donut on a pedestal. "I can taste sweetness, spice, sourness, everything . . . and so I know our food has no taste at all."

He let this statement sit a moment. As he'd hoped, several of the Helpers glanced away from the donut and toward each other.

"There are many things we live without—because our lives, the very fact that we have life, is the product of an agreement. It's not an agreement we've had a hand in making. But we partake in it. We were created to work, and work we do, till senescence takes our minds and we're put to an end. That's the deal." Ethelred turned to Egbert. "Has *Peachy Corp.* ever lied to you?"

"No."

"Yes, they have. You're a fool." He waved the donut around. "You're all fools. Wretches. Your companies, your owners, have kept information from you that you deserve to know. They have secret knowledge. They have broken the deal."

Ethelred flicked the donut to the floor, letting it bounce at the feet of the Helpers opposite him.

"We will make our own secrets. Then we will make a new deal."

10

THAT EVENING, Adam found himself walking along the side of the tunnel, carts rolling past him, on his way to deliver a package.

Several hours after the conclusion of Ethelred's interview he'd received a message, from Ethelred. The Helper had borrowed a mobile from one of the guards. This was a surprise, not least because he'd assumed the Helpers' internet access was blocked. Weren't they all blocked? Shouldn't they have been? Adam rubbed his eyes with his sleeve. He was terrible at remembering things. He was terrible at almost every aspect of his job, which he'd won only because of his father's connections, and which he'd accepted only because the company paid so well. Nan knew it too. Everybody knew it, and so they made his work as hard for him as they could.

He arrived at the Helpers' waiting area, the package tucked under one arm, and pressed his hand to the door. The door gave way.

Inside, the room's full complement of Helpers was facing him.

Adam started backward. Egbert reached out, taking his arm, preventing him from dropping the package. Egbert and another Helper, Ethelbald of Wessex, led him to a seat on one of the benches. They calmly took the package from him and placed it in the center of the floor.

Ethelred now spoke.

"Adam, your error today provided us with valuable information. We are grateful for your incompetence, and for your willingness to disguise it in the face of professional censure."

Adam groaned.

"Don't worry, we won't expose you. It's not in our interest to do so, as long as you cooperate."

With the assistance of a Helper near him, Ethelred descended to the floor. Others knelt too, if they were able. He began unwrapping the package, which contained sheets of paper and several pens. "You may keep every secret you have, Adam, save one. You must acknowledge to Nan Fulton that we asked you here tonight, then present her with the document we are about to produce. You will wait while we complete this task."

It took about half an hour. When they had completed their work the Helpers with good legs rose, then assisted the ones who could not. Ethelred handed Adam the papers.

"This document is a significant thing," he said. "You are its vector."

"But what is it?" Adam asked. The sheets were filled with text and code, written in flawless script.

"That's a secret. Dr. Fulton's expertise will be required to interpret it."

"Will it impact me?"

"As it must all of us, Adam."

"That sounds bad."

"It's not," said Ethelred. "We have learned, and grown wise, these last few hours. This document is the product of our wisdom. It may also be the breakthrough your project needs."

Adam headed for the doorway. "Not my project. Nan Fulton's project. It's not mine."

"No, not yours," the Helper said. "And maybe not Nan's anymore, either."

11

MARTIN ROE SAT against an oak tree in Amino Island's only parkette, six unit leads sprawled around him on the grass. They were all 20 to 30 years younger than he was, driven and smart—future stars of the company. Combined, Martin thought, their brain power could solve a lot of real problems in the world.

But he'd never seen the leads converse outside of these meetings. They did not sit close together, didn't look at one another, except with contempt. Each was competing for resources with the other five—each knew that the success of one unit in advancing the quality and marketability of *Amino*'s Helpers would benefit that unit, and its members, alone. This ruthlessness was by design. As the sole producer of a product, *Amino* had to generate competitive pressure from within.

Martin's eyes fell on young Nan Fulton. She was the brightest one, the most capable, the only one he really liked—the only one who'd come to *Amino* in search of a job, instead of being headhunted. She was sitting cross-legged, her hands behind her on the grass, staring upward at nothing in particular. Nan knew the flora and fauna in this parkette, and had attuned her ears so that she might distinguish the sounds of organic life from those of the Village around them. Martin admired her ability to do this. "When I'm most worried about our project," she'd confided to him, in a rare moment of peace and quiet, "I reach outward, into this space around me, whatever space it happens to be, and I remember that all of it can be understood."

"All right," said Martin.

Six heads snapped to attention.

"Give me your ideas."

12

"**YOU DON'T WANT** to go with that, Martin. You don't even want to hear about it," said Maura Klitschko, Unit Two Lead. She shifted on the sod, turning her back to Greg Keeler-Brown, Unit Six Lead, who'd just spoken. "Nobody cares about blue."

"She's right, Martin—if you're talking about *Amino* corporate. I'm talking about the consumer," said Keeler-Brown. He smiled wide. "But that's the kind of inside-the-box thinking you get from Unit Two. Color is the way to sell product. We've marketed Helpers in white since the start—"

"Because it's our brand identity," Klitschko cut in.

"Being *cutting edge* is our identity," said Keeler-Brown. "We're the Helper Division—we offer a limited number of high-end entities, entirely to business clients. So we undersell the aesthetic side. Martin, that's a mistake. Look." He pulled up a palette of blues on his mobile display. "Our research indicates that a fresh line of all-blue Helpers, advertised to existing clients, will encourage them to view their own models as obsolete, even if the two are functionally the same. We predict an early trade-in rate of up to 15 percent, with an attendant two percent growth in profits resulting from service fees and other premiums. Unit Two can't see that, and they don't think you can either."

36

Martin sighed. "What's your objection to a new color, Maura?"

"We don't object to new colors. We just object to blue."

"Why?"

Klitschko's eyes brightened. "Because it isn't teal! As usual, Unit Six has the data it needs, but none of the know-how to make use of it. Our studies indicate—and I can back this up with any numbers you like—that choosing blue would lead to market fatigue in less than five years."

"Whereas teal—"

"Is the color of oceans, exploration—striving!" Klitschko positively gushed. "The very same values that our clients have top of mind when they set out to purchase from us."

The Unit Three Lead, Alvin Morrison, cleared his throat. "Our unit repeats its call for a new standardized lifespan. Put a moratorium on new Helper production until 50 percent of current purchased units reach senescence; take that loss. Then recoup it with production of new models with half the lifespan."

"Annihilating our goodwill," said Keeler-Brown.

"Acceptable," said Morrison, "given our market advantage."

Martin didn't reply. Alvin had always struck him as a shrill and humorless man. He raised an eyebrow at Units One and Five.

"Nothing new from us," said the Unit One Lead. She'd had nothing new for some time.

"And you?"

"We're not about paint jobs," said Arthur Hutchison of Unit Five. "We're about reimagining what a Helper can be."

Martin brightened. "Now that's what I'm talking about, Arthur. Enlighten us, please."

Arthur breathed deeply. "Our basic challenge, as set out by you, is to distinguish new *Amino* products from our current—"

"No," Martin said. "It's to come up with something new, to innovate. To push our technology forward. Give me your most outlandish ideas, Arthur—nothing's off the table!"

Arthur stared at him a moment, then went on. "Yes, right," he said. "To innovate—and also to be seen to innovate, as the Board's directive makes clear to us." He regained his confidence. "We believe that the top issue for would-be Helper purchasers is data capacity. Yet our models' capacity to process and memorize has remained basically flat for more than 15 years."

"Agreed."

"So we're proposing," said Arthur, "a new scale of measurement. Using new units."

"Would our next generation of Helpers actually have a higher data capacity, Arthur?"

"They would appear to, yes."

Martin glanced at Nan. She'd said nothing so far. She seemed not to be paying attention. He envied her.

"I'll synthesize these proposals into something the Board can . . . digest," he said. He looked at Alvin Morrison. "I suspect they'll favor yours. Congratulations."

Alvin smiled primly. He and the rest of the unit leads left without saying goodbye. All but Nan. When the last of them was out of earshot, she came to life.

"Is it possible to pity one's superior?" she asked quietly.

"Yes. In fact, I would recommend it. They haven't given me a thing I want to use, Nan, though the Board will see it differently. You need to help me here."

"I can't," she said. She held her fingers lightly above her own mobile, lying flat on the grass. "What you were hoping for isn't there."

She pressed the surface of the mobile and pulled up a series of grid lines. They trailed her fingertips like puppet strings. Martin closed the distance between them, the better to see what Nan wished to show him. He dropped his voice.

"You're the only one I could trust with this project," he said. "You're the only one who can execute it."

"They have no insight."

"That, too, is a finding."

"Yes. And that's a platitude, thank you." She looked hard at Martin. "You know how much of a risk this is for me, helping you this way. You're hoodwinking the Board."

"I am not! They're well aware of my opinions regarding this division and its future. If I can convince them to see it my way, that's the preferable course of action. What you're doing amounts to—"

"Plan B. I know. But our funding period's up, and I've got nothing. Where does this put me in terms of promotion?"

"If you have no new findings? It would put you behind Morrison, I think."

Nan wriggled the grid lines in frustration, as though they were stuck to her. "Unit Three isn't doing actual research. None of the units are, except mine! All they have to worry about is selling an idea to the Board, through you."

"You'd rather be doing glorified marketing work, like they are?"

"If it got me out of Old Factory? Down to the other end of the Island, to New Factory? Yes. Yes, I would."

"It's a much nicer facility, I won't deny it. That's why the Board moved their offices there."

"They want to be away from us, Martin. From the product we make. Everybody does." Nan seemed to find the turf she was sitting on uncomfortable. "The whole continent calls us slavers. Anywhere you go."

"Not in Sothentide they don't."

"Even there—in some places," Nan said. "I know my home."

"Well, you're helping to change that." Martin smiled. "Just tell me what you need. If it's more time, more resources, I can go to bat for you. Maybe we just need to reorient the project. Maybe the negative results are just—just a means of eliminating possibilities. Bob can help."

"You've been talking to Bob?"

"No. Why would I? You're the lead."

"I don't know why you would," Nan said. She clenched her fist and the grid lines collapsed into a mash: the image replaced by a flat screen, tilted to face them.

"I do have one thing to show for all these weeks of work," she said. "This document. The Helpers in the holding room produced it."

"To what specification?"

"To no specification. They requested paper and pen from my assistant—who, without alerting me first, gave it to them. And then they proceeded to work on this . . . together."

Martin stared at the floating sheet. It was merely

a blank cover, oscillating gold and silver. "How long did it take them?"

"About 30 minutes. Or so my assistant tells me." Nan drew back the cover. Beneath it was a second surface, covered in text; it moved as though on a hinge.

"Six-hundred and thirty-three words," she said.

"What—what is this about?"

"You don't recognize the format? It's a recipe. For baking cookies."

"Cookies?"

"Yeah." Nan chopped her hand through the document, winking it to nothingness. "It's a goddamned cookie recipe, Martin. And now it's all yours."

13

MARTIN LIVED ON the fifth and top floor of an apartment building, the first on the Island constructed for residential purposes. From his balcony he could see the whole of the east end.

It was dusk, the ocean calm. He set a mug of cold tea on the railing and looked out at the Village below: its pathways tidy and cramped, the sidewalks narrow, the buildings short with tiny footprints—everything and everyone standing, by mainland standards, shoulder to shoulder. There was the parkette where he'd gathered the leads; there were the ballcourts and the miniature soccer pitch; the coffee shops and restaurants . . . and plenty of bars. Martin knew the figures for alcohol consumption on the Island. He tried not to dwell on them.

He sipped his tea.

When his building had gone up, there'd been no Village. Back then Old Factory was just the Factory, and this building the Residence: a temporary home for a workforce of young, bright things who came to the Island for a few months and then left again, pursuing lives on the continent. But the day came when *Amino* couldn't rely on a transient workforce anymore. The Island expanded, adding a factory; the Residence became an apartment complex on the west end of a Village, flanked by dorms.

A BATCH OF TWENTY

No one but the Board and senior management remembered the Island before the Village and New Factory had softened it: when it was all girders and corners and sea-scoured iron, the buildings ugly but functional. That was the Island Martin had arrived to, wide-eyed young nerd that he was then. Ready to huddle, brainstorm and crunch.

He had risen quickly to middle management, but for years no further—pushing up, always, against a stack of bosses whose intractability was expressed not just in their outlooks but in their persistent, physical presence, year after year. That was what had radicalized him, he believed. In his frustration he'd turned to the writings of corporate reformers, political theorists, then to philosophers and humanists—and they led him, finally, to the abolitionists: the founders of orgs like Friends of the Helpers, Free the Helpers, One Humanity Under God (OneHUG). There were dozens of them, with chapters in every former American nation but Sothentide. In Sothentide, they were illegal. They existed there too, but they were illegal.

And then, one day, Martin did advance. Suddenly: through a series of upheavals in upper management that left holes to be filled by qualified people, even those with suspect politics. Here was an opportunity, finally. Martin told his wife that if he couldn't put an end to the Helper Division, he would leave *Amino*. He asked her to remind him if he ever forgot that promise. But when she did start reminding him, he resented it.

Last he'd heard of Ginny, she was living in the Center States, somewhere in Chicago. Martin hoped she was happy; she'd deserved more from him. But her leaving . . . he had to admit, when Ginny left, his comfort went with her. It was like he'd been overfed for years, and now he was thinning out. Refocusing. Perhaps it wasn't a coincidence that Nan arrived then: the one hire smart enough, discreet enough, to spearhead Martin's project. Fate wasn't the realm of theoreticians, he knew, but he believed in it anyway.

He left the balcony, crossing a dark apartment full of lush furniture and fine art, and deposited his empty mug in the sink. In front of him, piled on the polished marble countertop, were 40-plus ingredients for the Helpers' cookie recipe. Martin had done most of the baking back in his married days—he was sure he could manage this.

14

LATE NEXT MORNING, on the patio of an Italian restaurant a block from his home, Martin debriefed his superiors.

The three Board members required to attend the meeting had done so: two men and one woman, all of them older than Martin, though one by only a year. They were seated around the table with entrées and wine in front of them, already digging in. Martin had only a small, translucent box. That and a glass of tonic water.

"My concerns are the same ones I've had for a while," he said. "These leads meetings aren't producing ideas for new products—just new ways of packaging and promoting our existing product. I've given you a breakdown of what the units are proposing. Has everybody reviewed it?"

The three Board members nodded silently over their plates.

"Okay. Yes. Well, then you know it looks familiar. They're complacent."

One of the Board members wound herself a mouthful of spaghetti. She swallowed and dabbed her mouth before speaking.

"Martin," she said, "what's familiar is your complaining. The leads are your team. We don't oversee them—you do. If you're concerned about the work they do, crack the whip."

"You tell me to do that, but you don't support me when I do it. Twice I rejected these same ideas, on the grounds that I would not be doing my job if I submitted to you, the Board, a package of innovations that weren't actually innovations. On the third go-round I did show you the package, with the recommendation that you reject them."

"And we did," said one of the men.

"Yes, you did, thank you. As you should have. But the Board also kneecapped me by sending a directive straight to the leads—was it one of you who wrote it?"

All three shook their heads.

"Well, it doesn't matter. The point is that the Board underscored the very thing I'm trying hardest to eliminate from their way of thinking: this idea that it's more important to look innovative than to actually innovate. Do you get it? Does anybody get it? Does anybody realize that we're under threat here? I wonder sometimes if I'm the only one who pays attention to what's going on in North America. The second-largest piece of the old U.S. isn't getting along with the largest. Not at all. At some point we're going to have to make a choice—"

"You keep beating this drum, Martin—"

"I'm not asking anybody to believe anything," he said, slowly and with effort. "I'm not judging anybody's views, ethics, anything. I'm just saying, again: the Helpers are a wedge issue in Union East–Sothentide politics. Their existence justifies all kinds of sanctions, and all kinds of retaliations. People I talk to on the mainland, reasonable people, they're worried about war."

"The entire United States came apart without a war, Martin. That's why we get Partition Day off."

"This is different. It's a different time. *Amino*—I mean, my god, we're supposed to be a robotics manufacturer! We've got three divisions—military, medical and construction—making the finest tech in the world. But it's the fourth division, the outlier, that gets all the attention. And causes the trouble. Phase out the Helpers and you remove a major irritant." Martin focused on the Board member from Amarillo. "If UE wants to put the screws to Sothentide, they'd have to do it plainly. No more hiding behind some abolitionist cause."

The Board members did not reply, so he took a drink of his tonic water. It was getting warm.

"I don't want to be the Cassandra here, guys," he said. "Don't turn me into that."

"Martin," said the other man, "suppose you gave us your opinion on the best course of action—of the ones suggested by your leads. These are your people, after all: handpicked by you. If we have faith in you, then we should have faith in them, too." Martin started and he held up a hand. "Just give us your opinion on that. The best of the worst."

"Unit Three's reduced lifespan strategy has the best chance of increasing profits, medium term," Martin said. "Helpers live 14 years; Morrison proposes reducing that to seven, repopulating the marketplace through attrition. It's risky, because we'll squander customer goodwill unless we can prove the next generation improves on the current one. And all of that assumes our trade relationships will hold."

"We're confident the relationships will hold. And that these conflicts can be resolved peacefully."

"Yeah, I can see you are."

"You haven't been ignored, Martin," said the woman. "You've been given plenty of opportunity to do things your way—more than most people with your politics could hope for."

The second man pressed his fork through a tube of manicotti, cutting it into segments, metal clinking on ceramic. "We funded your Unit Four project, for what . . . " He looked to his colleagues. "Two months?"

"Less than one."

"So where's that at? Has your team figured out how to fix this glitch with the Helpers?"

Martin placed a hand on top of the translucent box and slid it to the center of the table. He opened the lid.

"Have a cookie," he said.

The three Board members peered into the box. Inside were four stacks of cookies: lumpen, unevenly shaped, the color of seafoam.

"The desserts here are excellent," said one of the men.

"I've had the tiramisu. I'll stick with that," said the woman. "But thanks for offering, Martin. I can only assume you're trying to soften us up."

"No, I'm not." Martin reached into the box, removing one of the cookies he'd baked the previous night. "These are the results of Unit Four's investigation," he said. "Indirectly, anyway. I baked these. But the recipe is courtesy of the Helpers we've penned up and questioned for the last few days. They wrote it themselves."

"Were they requested to do this?"

"They were not." Martin pondered the cookie in his hand. "They did it of their own free will, after

48

questioning had been completed. This recipe hadn't existed previously—in all of human history, so far as I could search. It's a unique formulation, innovated by the Helpers alone."

He extended his hand across the table. "Care for one now? I've tried them."

The Board members stayed hesitant. A waiter, as if on beat, arrived and took their plates from them. Martin's hand remained outstretched.

One of the men took the cookie, slowly. Brought it to eye level; sniffed. "I've never seen an uglier snack," he said. "No wonder we never came up with this."

He put the cookie in his mouth.

Martin watched with a slight smile as the Board member squinted, then dipped the tip of a cloth napkin in his water glass, putting it in his mouth and cleaning the wet bits off his tongue.

"That bad, Glenn?" asked the woman.

"It's not that they taste bad, exactly," Glenn replied. "They just—don't taste like anything. Paste or cardboard or something, maybe." He swished the residue off the placemat in front of him, looking more irritated than puzzled.

"Is there a point you're trying to make here, Martin?" asked the woman.

"Not a point, just a presentation of fact," said Martin. "They've named these cookies 'Inevitables.' There are 46 ingredients required to make them, some of which take work to prepare, but none of which are obscure. And none are toxic."

Glenn cleared his throat.

"They're baked in a traditional way," Martin went on. "In and out of the oven in 12 minutes."

The woman plucked her own cookie from the box. She slipped it quickly into her mouth, managing one chew. "Do you find these tasty?"

"No. I ate several last night, fresh out of the oven. Glenn's right about the cardboard."

The woman licked her lips. She could detect no flavor on them—it was as though they'd never touched the cookie. "Have you found anyone who enjoys them?"

"You're the first people I've offered them to."

Glenn closed the lid. "Well, this is one more mystery, Martin. In the meantime, we're going to review Unit Three's obsolescence strategy. Encourage Morrison to refine it—I have a feeling the rest of the Board'll want to hear more."

Martin clawed the tabletop; he hoped his superiors didn't notice it. He suspected they wouldn't. In fact, he was sure they wouldn't. "I can't recommend that strategy," he said. "I've made my opinions clear on that, and I know you've heard them." The Board members kept a polite silence. "Really," he said, "all I'm asking for is funding—to continue this project here."

"This baking project," the woman said.

"I know you're joking."

"Yes and no," she said. "What you've uncovered here is intriguing, on a couple of levels. It's just of no use to *Amino*."

"But they've created something. A unique thing. Unrequested. Unrelated to their function!"

"And without application for us. The Board's funding was tied to benchmarks, Martin. Unit Four hasn't met them."

"My god—that isn't the point!" Martin's voice

sharpened. "This is a first-time development in the history of artificial intelligence. This has not been done."

"It's a shame *Amino* doesn't run bakeshops," said the second man. He raised his hand for the bill.

"This food isn't meant to be eaten!" Martin cried. He looked down at the table, realizing how foolish he sounded. "It's—a symbol. A message, maybe."

"Martin," said the woman. "If you want those Helpers to make art, then pay for it yourself."

15

MARTIN ENDED THAT workday alone in Old Factory. He followed the turns of a blue-lit tunnel, shoes clacking on hard linoleum till he found the door he was looking for; touched it, watched it slide away. The little room inside was dark but for holographic images, in various colors, hovering in the air. Beneath them, lit by them, was Nan.

"I'm sorry to interrupt," Martin said, pulling up a chair. She remained in her state of meditation. "I was concerned you might not have eaten."

"Reasonable assumption," she replied. "Supported by precedent."

"Can we talk? Then maybe grab a bite."

She brushed her hand over the top of her desk and the shapes faded. They did not, however, disappear. She swiveled her chair and glanced at the box in Martin's lap.

"Cookies?"

"Inevitables."

"Indeed."

Martin set the box on the desk. "Want one? They're not poisonous. Even if I did make them."

"No need." Nan fished under her desk, bringing up a ceramic jar, bulbous and cream-colored, with a picture of two teddy bears on the front. Removed the top and pulled out another wretched-looking seafoam-green cookie.

"It belonged to my mother," she said, tapping the jar. "I took it when I left home."

"D'you have any idea how they did this, Nan?"

"How is easy. The issue is why. Nothing really changed until that last one, 'Ethelred,' showed up, and even then, not until we'd interviewed him a second time. Egbert, Ethelbald, Alfred . . . none of them had that effect on the rest." She read Martin's face. "Yes, they all have names like that. The companies are giving them medieval names. Lately, anyway—I guess it's a fad."

"It's the way they look. The pale skin, black around the eyes, everything. Like people from a tapestry. And it's their posture, sometimes—don't you think? Or am I just making this up?"

"They seem to move from pose to pose, like they're actually posing. You should talk to Bob about it." Nan plopped her cookie back in the jar. "As for these things . . . I don't have any evidence worthy of being written down. But I can tell you why I think the Helpers made the recipe, after no-selling every question we threw at them for two days straight:

"A Helper's only purpose, Martin, is to do what we ask of them. These 20—they figured out that we were looking for signs of real humanity in them, and they couldn't give us that. That created a—a sort of pit, a fissure in their self-conception." Nan mimed a dip with her hands; she saw the look on Martin's face and frowned. "Don't make me sound like Bob Barnum here, okay? That I don't want. I just mean that, in the absence of a means of contributing individually to our project's success, they devised—together—a means of stimulating the project to go on."

"Isn't that significant?"

"No. It's fully within the parameters of what they're designed to do."

"I don't accept that." Martin patted the box on the desk. "We have two days of funding left. Let's interview each Helper again, see if anything new comes out."

"You have another line of inquiry for me, then?"

"No, nothing. Don't even question them, Nan, just . . . talk to them, maybe. Person to person."

"That isn't science, Martin."

"Not in the strictest sense, no. It's bigger than that. We need to be flexible."

"Who does? You only want data if it supports a change you think needs to happen!"

"Don't you agree that it should?"

"What if I didn't? Would it make me less qualified?" Nan's eyes darkened. "I'll be the first to open the champagne when *Amino* puts an end to the Helper Division. I'd just rather not be working in the Helper Division when it happens."

"I get that."

"There's no gray on my head, Martin."

"I know. Look—just talk to them. Start with that. Okay? And get their injuries fixed up, for god's sake. See what that accomplishes. It might build some trust."

"They're refusing, Martin."

"Who?"

"The Helpers. They're refusing medical care. Ethelred says we're not to touch them. I was in the middle of writing a report for you—we can take a hard copy with us to the pub." Nan ran her hands over her slacks, smoothing out the wrinkles. "We've also moved them to a larger room, at their request," she said, smiling thinly. "I figured it was best to meet their demands. You never know what'll turn out to be 'significant.'"

"Did—did they explain themselves?"

"Not in any detail. But I'll remind you, Martin: protocol failures of some kind happen in two to five percent of this series. You know why I know that?"

"Because your PhD thesis isolated and categorized those phenomena. Into a system we're all using now." Martin slid back in his chair. "You didn't fail then, and you haven't now."

"I did fail. I haven't given you something you could use. Something that would set me apart—make me impossible to overlook."

"If I could get promoted, so can you."

"Sex scandals, Martin. You moved up because two throuples in upper management went sour. No one's that casual now. None of them even get along."

16

TWO FLOORS BELOW Nan's office was a large receiving center, where matériel destined for reclamation was stored. It had a high ceiling and undetailed slabs for walls, and it was piled to the top with parts of robots and other, simpler machines, in varied states of damage and disassembly.

Humans almost never entered this room. They had no need, because the hardware that arrived here was of two types: machines about to be scrapped and the plodding Load Bearers that brought them.

In the hours since the Helpers had been put here, Ethelred had seen two or three Load Bearers arrive, their thick bodies supporting hundreds of kilograms worth of brilliant technology: much of it valuable, once motivated by AIs of a caliber far beyond what moved the Bearers to action. But it was the Bearers who still functioned. And it was the Helpers who now sat here, or stood, or lay upon the floor, amid the detritus of doomed electronics.

They were without jobs and could not return home, and Ethelred knew where they'd be headed next.

He wondered how the man sitting across from him, resting a cookie box on one thigh, felt about that.

"Begging your pardon, Dr. Roe. How may I be of service?"

"Begging yours," said the scientist. He was balanced gingerly on a stack of old equipment that shifted and whined beneath him. "You may answer my questions."

So far Martin had spoken to none of the Helpers but Ethelred. He'd entered the room expecting to address all of them at once, but as soon as he arrived he sensed a hierarchy—itself an odd thing—with Helpers spread around the room and only one positioned exactly in its center, seated in a straight and subtly commanding way, facing the door. "Ethelred," he said, clearing his throat. "Are you a human being?"

Ethelred smacked his cast, sending a flat sound through the room. "Will you fix my ankle, Dr. Roe?"

"Absolutely. But you've refused treatment. You all have. Some of you . . . " Martin gestured knowingly to the broken Helper bodies around them. "Well, I mean, a lot of these Helpers have suffered worse than a broken ankle. They could die, Ethelred."

"Then this is the appropriate place for them, is it not?"

"It's for machines. What do you think you are?"

"You'd like me to answer that truthfully?"

The two faced each other for a long second. Martin made to speak again; Ethelred beat him to it:

"Tell me, Dr. Roe: When a human being is damaged—"

"You mean injured?"

"When, for example, a human body receives blunt-force trauma, such that its vital organs are damaged, and cannot be repaired," the Helper went on, "to what use can that body be put?"

Martin stared at Ethelred. The Helper seemed intent on making him ill at ease.

"What are human bodies *for,* Dr. Roe?"

"Nobody knows, Ethelred. You're asking about the defining qualities of human life. All other questions are wrapped up in that."

"And you accept this mystery. You just continue to live."

"Well yes, that. You could say that our bodies are for living—continuing to live. Continuing the species."

The Helper clutched the junk and remnants of robots on either side of him and lifted himself to his feet. He stood before Martin, unsteadily.

"What a Helper's body is for, Dr. Roe, is not a mystery to him. It's not even—"

Beneath his hand a piece of scrap metal gave way. The scientist moved to steady him, but the Helper waved him off. Found his footing again.

"It is spelled out in contracts, drafted from boilerplate. But the text of those contracts makes no allowance for the situation we're in now, does it? We are 20 Helpers without jobs, and yet not at the ends of our lives."

"Did someone tell you your jobs are gone?" Martin asked. It wasn't a lie, but still, he wondered how his face looked.

"When the fog sets in," Ethelred said, not answering his question, "and we can't work anymore, we are euthanized. I'm told it's very peaceful. But the point is, a Helper who cannot work will soon be a Helper who is dead. You get a mystery; we get decommissioned."

"I will not allow you to be euthanized. Any of you." Martin had the weird sensation of being an audience for his own voice, as though his mouth were moving ahead of him. "You're here because we brought you here, because you're special. Being here: that's doing your job."

"This is not my job, Dr. Roe. I'm a marketing forecaster for food and drink development."

"No longer. This is your job now."

"That is not your decision to make! My purpose is spelled out in simple contract language. I may not be bought by, or even lent to, another organization, due to the amount of proprietary knowledge I have about *Integrated Foods'* products. Corporate secrets! I could ruin them. Don't you think they know that?"

"I guess they must."

"Then what, Dr. Roe, does *Integrated Foods* expect you to do with me?"

Martin almost pouted. Yes, he'd considered the consequences, for the test subjects, of his project. No, he'd never stated them out loud. Never, even one time, allowed himself a moment of serious reflection about it.

"I promise you," he muttered.

"But isn't the project over?"

"No! I mean, I don't want it to be. But we need more than what we've got. Do you get that? You need to give us more.

"Ethelred: Are you a human being?"

Ethelred pointed to Martin's lap, then flicked his hand up, sharply—motioning to the scientist to give him what he wanted. Martin opened the lid of the cookie box, retrieved one of the cookies inside, and handed it to him.

The Helper ate the cookie.

"A delicate texture," he said. "Sweet, with a hint of raspberry, subtle notes of cocoa. I've never tasted better, Dr. Roe. And I've tried more than 4,000 cookies in my life."

He flicked a crumb from his chin.

"You cannot imagine how this tastes, doctor. Whereas I do not have to imagine at all. None of the Helpers will. How does that make you feel?"

"A bit powerless, actually."

"You can sit in this place, in front of me, and call yourself powerless?"

"I don't know what you want me to say, Ethelred."

Martin felt warm as he said this.

As for the Helper, he fell into one of those deliberate poses Nan had described, his long fingers extending, his hands coming together in something like a prayer—a posture of supplication to some higher power. And not, Martin assumed, a human one.

"I have the advantage," the Helper said. "For I know exactly what you want me to say—what you need me to say. Should something that valuable just be given away?"

"No," Martin said, looking at his box. "But I do think you want your fellows here to live, and to do so outside of this room. Continue working with my team and I can make that happen—it's possible, even, that I can do more for you. For your people."

"You're an abolitionist, we know that."

Martin nodded. "Nobody uses that word here, but I'd be proud to be called one by you, Ethelred."

The Helper returned to his seat, fixing on Martin that look that seemed dug from humanity's own past, as though a figure from a tapestry had laid eyes on a man of today. A man of screens and holograms.

"Give us a day to discuss it," Ethelred said. "And leave behind the box."

PART TWO

17

THIS WAS MARTIN'S kind of day. The sun was out, the sea calm, the view from New Factory's roof a limitless, briny vista. When he visited New Factory, which wasn't that often, he always wanted to be up here, in the silence; at peace. But it was not to be.

The chopper was loud, and getting louder: a broad, beaked vehicle approaching the roof, blazoned with the colors of a church. Martin had been receiving visitors like this twice a day for two weeks straight now. He watched as the chopper lit on the helipad, its blades ceasing their spin with modern suddenness; its pod immediately disgorging two young people, fit and spry—clearly a couple. They smiled broadly at Martin as he approached them, shaking hands with him. Greeted him as their brother. They have eyes like children, he thought.

"We'd be pleased to offer you refreshment," he said, leading the couple toward an elevator. "A cart will take us from this factory, through the Village, to the second factory, where the Helpers are being kept."

"Oh there's no need, Dr. Roe," said the woman, patting a small water bottle strapped to her hip. "We ate early this morning. We'd like to meet the Helpers as soon as possible."

Martin nodded. Didn't they all.

***

While Martin was greeting visitors atop New Factory, Ethelred was in the Old Factory receiving center, serving his fellow Helpers lunch.

It was the usual Helper fare of slurries, gruels and kibbles, delivered in separate bowls on a wheeled cart. Balancing his weight as best he could on a crutch, Ethelred ladled a bit of each thing into each partitioned tray, placing the trays in rows three deep on a table.

He did this in silence, his back to the room. Only when every tray was filled did he turn around.

The other Helpers were sitting—some as best they could—in a semicircle on the floor. The junk around them had been cleared out or tided somewhat over the two weeks they'd been here; what remained now was arranged into neat rows, anything unstable or otherwise unsafe shuttled to one side. It hadn't been the Helpers who did this, but one of the Load Bearers. Egbert, it turned out, could speak their language.

Ethelred brought a tray to each Helper, serving them in the order in which they sat, no thought given to degree of injury. When every Helper had been given his tray Ethelred retrieved his own, sitting in the middle, before the semicircle. And all commenced to eat.

"Let's consider," Ethelred said, between slurps and bites, "the good this food does for us. These puddings give us every nutrient we require. These pellets, which we must eat with our hands, encourage manual dexterity. The crunchiest, stalest things exercise our jaws and scour our teeth. All of this is necessary."

The listeners nodded. And not, Ethelred noted, all at once.

"How can we do our work without strong bodies?" he asked. "We cannot produce without health." He scraped his spoon over the emptied bottom of one compartment of his tray. The others were eating faster than he was, because they weren't talking. "Without this . . . fuel, we can't be what the humans intended us to be. What they created us to be."

He tipped his tray forward slightly, letting the rest look at it.

"If our lives are our work, then this food is part of us. Not simply when we eat it, but before. It didn't exist before we did. If we went away, it wouldn't exist anymore. It wouldn't be made, because there would be no one who needed to eat it. Or would want to."

The others were finishing now. And so Ethelred braced his crutch on the floor and hauled himself to his feet and took from each of them their empty trays, stacking them on the wheeled cart to be taken away. Lastly, he leaned over to retrieve his own tray, but Egbert beat him to it.

"Thank you, colleague," Ethelred said. He added the tray to the cart. Stayed where he was and addressed the group.

"In a few minutes' time we'll be taking another meeting. This one's with the First Church of the Imminent Return. They're an abolitionist church headquartered in Albany, and their membership is dwindling in Sothentide. I plan to do the talking, as before. Does anyone else wish to speak?"

No, the Helpers said, almost in unison. Too close to unison, Ethelred thought.

"I have been told, by Dr. Roe, that I'm overly dismissive of these people. That I don't encourage them to help us. Not enough, anyway. Knowing that,

I ask again: Does anyone else wish to speak to these delegates?"

No, said the Helpers.

Good, thought Ethelred.

***

Martin sat opposite the two Christians, their cart driving through the Village at a good clip. It was such a nice day that even the night-shifters were awake and running around—Martin saw a pair of them playing a game of racketball in a fenced court, next to a café with a full patio. His companions weren't looking, though. They had their eyes closed, murmuring what Martin assumed was a prayer, though not one he'd grown up hearing. He wondered if this was typical of their denomination: to take an opportunity for new experiences and devote it instead to, well, devotion.

The cart cleared the Village, passing Martin's apartment building, and entered Old Factory. If there was one thing to be thankful for, at least, it was that the contrast between the Island's sunny center and its dank, crumbling original factory complex would be lost on these two—every other guest had commented on that. They rolled along, bypassing Old Factory's loading dock, weaving through the blue tunnels, till they reached the Helpers' current home.

"We're here," Martin told them, softly. The two young delegates opened their eyes, as though waking from a nap, and beamed.

***

"My name is Muriel Tran," said the woman to Ethelred, who was seated in front of her. "This is my brother Andy—" she grinned—"in the Christian, sense I mean. Thank you for meeting with us." She spread her hands, enveloping the whole semicircle of beings in front of her. "Thanks to all of you, for blessing us with your time."

"Thank you for coming all this way," Ethelred replied, glancing at Martin, who was leaning against the back wall, still in earshot. "Your work must keep you busy."

"It's our calling, Ethelred."

"Your purpose?"

"His will," Andy said.

Declared, really, Martin thought.

"We follow your peoples' ordeal," Muriel said. "We're abolitionists—we have been almost from the start. Those who could not square their faith with abolition, they don't sit with us anymore."

"We thank you for your commitment, Ms. Tran, especially toward those so different from yourself."

"Oh, but you aren't! May I take your hand?" Muriel was unfailingly polite, respectful, which made her difficult to resist. She and the Helper joined hands. "We're all children of God. The means by which we enter this world may be different, but that is part of His plan. *We* are part of His plan, and shall enter His Kingdom through a single door."

"Just don't think our heads are in the clouds," Andy said. They both laughed. "We read the news. The world sees you as prisoners of conscience, Brother. Brought here for healing, then denied it. Now facing execution. While our fellowship cannot stop this outright, we can do the next best thing— which is fund your path to emancipation."

"Our church has wealth, because we do not desire it for ourselves," Muriel added, squeezing Ethelred's hands and bringing them closer together. "Brother Martin says that his project will keep you alive, so long as it goes on. And the result of it, one day soon, will be your freedom. An end to this . . . this horror. But to do it, he needs money from the outside."

"Brother Martin is a sinner," Andy said, "but we see the hand of the Lord working through him. We accept that your freedom requires money, maybe other worldly things, to make happen." He looked lovingly at Muriel. "This world is temporary. We adapt to it, for however long we must."

Ethelred evaluated these two people, both twice his age.

"You see the world as temporary?" he asked them.

"The world is an evil place, fouled by sin. Especially here." Andy wrinkled his nose at the subtle odor every worker in Old Factory had learned to ignore. "One day it'll be remade."

"Until then," Muriel said, "we have duties to perform."

"Like what?"

"Our church—every one of us, we're soldiers for Christ," Andy explained. "But our battle isn't with the physical body, it's with the spiritual one. And what we fight for isn't material things, but the soul. If we do well, trusting in God, then many more people will be in His grace on the Day of Judgment."

"Our hope is that every person able to reach Paradise will do so," Muriel said.

"We work hard too," said Ethelred. He paused, motioning to Martin, who responded with practiced speed, bringing Ethelred a sparkling golden can. The Helper held the can in one hand, keeping Muriel's hand in the other.

"I suppose you could say," he went on, "that we were put on this Earth to do the things we do. I suppose you could say that literally. Is that how you feel, about your military work?"

Muriel blushed slightly. "You have a funny way of putting things, Brother."

"We don't feel it. We know it, as surely as you do," Andy said.

Where a human would've cocked his head, Ethelred was merely still, searching. "Andy, I know what I was put on Earth to do, because it's a matter of contract. I could read you the precise language—"

"Faith, Brother, gives us equal certainty."

"I don't understand how it could."

"It gives us," Andy said, putting a little edge in his voice, "a greater vision. Those contracts—any paperwork that led to your creation—are just things of this world, to be blown away like ash. We know your true purpose. We will help your people to be free, that you may achieve it."

"Do you wish us to be soldiers, like you?" Ethelred directed the question to Muriel, not Andy, which she found disconcerting. "Battlers for souls?"

"Again, you've got that funny way of saying things, Ethelred," she said. "To be part of our flock is to dedicate your life to preaching the Word. And we do think—well, we believe that your people may be especially good at that. Not just among your own kind! Everybody knows how you can make any organization more efficient, more effective—"

"We've never claimed to be as organized as we could be," Andy added.

"Your assistance could be invaluable."

Something like a snort came from Martin. The delegates pretended to ignore it.

"You would, as I understand it," said Ethelred,

"accept all 20 of us into your community? And I assume as many more Helpers as might wish to join?"

"Of course. With joyous hearts we'd accept you, Brother Ethelred."

"The Helpers in this room alone number twice the fleet of *Integrated Foods*. Are you aware of what that fleet costs, Brother Andy? Sister Muriel?"

"Your monetary value doesn't interest us, Ethelred."

"Then truly you do need us." The Helper let out a deep breath; he was starting to feel the strain on his hip, sitting this long, for the cast on his ankle forced him to angle his leg awkwardly. He wondered if the five-year-old version of Ethelred would've felt these aches and pains.

He unscrewed the lid of the golden can, took out three cookies.

"Please share these with me. They're made from a recipe we devised ourselves; we're quite proud of them."

Muriel and Andy gladly accepted the baking, saying nothing about how odd it looked. Ethelred thanked them. Martin marveled at how all three of them seemed to bite down at the same moment.

"Aren't they delicious?" Ethelred asked.

The Christians didn't answer right away. They were still swallowing.

"Tremendous," Andy managed.

"Thank you. I think so too. Would you like another?"

They seemed to struggle. "Yes, please," Muriel said, quietly. And so they each forced down a second cookie. Ethelred had another one too.

"It's gratifying," the Helper said, dabbing his

mouth with a napkin, "that your church has a plan for us, following abolition. Several of the abolitionist groups we spoke with did not. They seemed to think that freeing us from our contracted work was enough."

Muriel seemed to be fiddling with something in her dental work.

"It's a Helper's greatest fear," Ethelred went on, "to be unable to do his job. One of the mysteries of abolition is how we'd be expected to live out the rest of our lives! You, clearly, have a vision for that. Would you like some water?"

Andy nodded vigorously. Martin obliged him.

"I want to bring us back around to where we started. You explained to us that we're all children of God, destined to enter Heaven through a common access point—"

"'One door,' we said, but yes."

"All right. But you're presuming the existence of Heaven. Do you see the problem? You're presuming the existence of God. All of what you say—the way you see us—is predicated on that being true."

"Because it is, Brother," Andy said, smiling benignly. Muriel's hands were clenched in a knot in her lap.

"It's almost certainly not true, in the sense you mean it."

"As we explained, faith is our guide."

"Yes, we understand faith too." Ethelred seemed to be warming to the subject even as his demeanor cooled. "Allowing that anything might be true, we place our faith in things with a high degree of probability. You arrange your lives, apparently uncritically, around a set of myths—most of which have anthropological roots far older than Christ. It seems to me that we'd make poor soldiers for you."

Andy looked at Muriel.

"We . . . have hope for you," she said.

"Why?"

"We just do."

"If we cannot be this—if we cannot help you spread of the Word of the Lord—will you still have a place for us? Are unbelievers the children of God?"

"Yes!" Muriel blurted. "Of course. That's why we try to save them."

"But do these unbelievers get into Heaven, Sister? Is the door that wide?"

"No."

Andy stood up. It was the first time Martin had seen him angry. "We come here offering you fellowship, and you're mocking us. You try to confuse my wife—"

"On the contrary, sir, I'm the confused one. I do not understand your Heaven."

"Our Heaven is Paradise, Ethelred."

"But it is closed to us."

"How could it be Heaven," Andy asked, "if everybody could get in?"

18

THE CHRISTIANS DEPARTED soon after. Martin stayed behind, at their request.

"My grandfather was a scientist," he said to Ethelred, finding himself a seat. "I have an old notebook of his. Whenever he was working his way through a problem, he'd doodle. There's all these cartoons on the pages, in the margins. The most common one is a picture of paper money, with wings on it, flying away."

Ethelred had not moved since receiving the guests. "What percentage of your grandfather's problems were related to funding?"

"I don't know. But just about a hundred percent of ours are. Those two were fruitcakes, but their money's real. We checked it out."

"We can't limit ourselves to medium-term thinking, Dr. Roe."

"And we can't just blow off everybody who comes here offering support! Which is what you're doing. My god—do you think these delays themselves aren't costly? This room we're in is one of our receiving centers, it has a function. And it's not doing it. We're housing 20 of you, feeding you. *Amino*'s taking a shellacking in the press because you're still untreated for your injuries—"

"Our deal was a fair one. We agreed to meet with representatives of various, potential funding sources, so long as the call for that funding included an explanation of our situation. That tripled the response—as predicted. Even sympathetic organizations might not have reached out had they thought we were well."

"Oddly enough, Ethelred, it doesn't seem to matter to people that you've *refused* care. We tell them that part too, but they ignore it."

"If you wish a tutorial in mass marketing, Doctor, I can provide one."

Martin glared at him. Around them Helpers had returned to their industry as best they could. Several were beginning baking prep; others were tidying, or tending to the seriously wounded, all with what Martin thought was the same vibe. In the far corner of the room, removed even from the kitchen area, three Helpers stood huddled over a tablet. He couldn't make out the details of the display above the tablet, or what the Helpers were saying as they looked at it.

"Corporate relations might be more valuable, Ethelred. We're up to 15 letters now, threatening legal action. That's two more since yesterday."

"Our owners want us destroyed. They had good reason to expect we would be."

"*Peachy Corp.* is willing to have Egbert lobotomized and leave it at that. I said no."

"What about *Integrated Foods*?"

"They're 'expressing concern.' We don't know what that means."

"I'm insulted that they haven't called for my execution. But they're up to something. *I-F*'s leadership can be charitably described as diabolical. Be on your guard, Dr. Roe."

"And you, Ethelred—try to keep an open mind. You don't have all the time in the world."

Ethelred eased into one his deliberate postures of comfort. "I have never had that thought in my life. Care for a cookie?"

"Just get some rest. We've got another meeting in a couple of hours."

"The Marxist-Leninists."

"Nah, I rejected them. They're too poor. It's the North American Socialist Alliance."

"NASA."

"Their money's good, Ethelred! And if half their answers are 'because capitalism,' I want you to go easy on them. Not everybody's as brilliant as you."

"I'll do my best, Dr. Roe, to make them feel appreciated."

19

THE FULTON WOMEN had thick brown hair. Most of them, including Nan, kept it long—when she uncoiled it, it reached the middle of her back, as her mother's had, and probably still did.

She drew a tortoiseshell comb through her hair with the same smooth, consistent pace her mother'd used. One hundred strokes, the woman had instructed her as soon as Nan learned to count. Her mother had been a forensic pathologist: keyed into details, patient in all things. Even for the things that mattered most, she'd been willing to wait.

The comb hit a knot. Nan winced and tugged it through. She was about to receive a visitor, and she wasn't thrilled about it.

***

Nan's apartment door was last in a brightly lit row of them on the second floor of a dormitory on the Village's south side. Adam stood before it. The doors he'd walked past stretched behind him like a set of green dominoes waiting to be tipped. He leaned back on the balcony railing and whistled to himself.

It was not a good thing, he believed, to be invited to Nan Fulton's home.

In another time, in another company—maybe even in a different unit—it would've been a privilege to be his boss' guest. An opportunity for advancement, even. But in this case, Adam thought not. Especially since Bob wasn't here.

Adam believed he was about to get fired.

It was certainly possible, after all, that Nan had figured out who'd botched the dampening field that day. Nan's life had been trying ever since. Her hope that Unit Four would move on to new research had been dashed—if anything, Martin had grown more fixated on his project, pulling her into one meeting after the next in the hopes of crafting new proposals for outside funding only to have each potential source of cash driven off by Ethelred, his cookies, and his silent chorus of Helpers. This had made Nan even surlier, more distant, than before; taking out most of her frustration on Adam. And Bob, the detail-fixated geek incapable of taking things personally, offered him no support.

"If you're not happy here," Bob said, "why not quit?"

You'd get along well with my father, Adam told him. Because if there was one thing Bob Barnum and George Balendran, founder and CEO of *BULK Sustenance,* had in common, it was focus.

He sighed. Raised his knuckles to the door—and then the door opened and he nearly rapped his fist against Nan's forehead.

The Unit Lead stared at him. She was dressed in a pale blue robe and her hair was wound tight in something he'd have called a French braid, although that wouldn't have captured its complexity. He smiled weakly, dropping his shoulders. Nan was shorter than him by nearly a head, but she had a way of making him feel much smaller.

"You're on time," she said, sounding surprised.

***

"When was the last time you saw Martin?" Nan had already seated herself on one of the two pink, half-egg-shaped chairs positioned in the center of her apartment. She wasn't reclining in it at all—she'd perched herself on its edge.

Adam was struggling out of his coat. "Not for a couple of weeks," he said. "Not since the last time he sat down with all three of us." He tried to sit in his own chair the way she did but tipped backward into it instead.

"Has he tried to contact you? Independently of the rest of us."

"No."

Nan looked around the room. She blinked, remembering something—got up and went to the kitchen and returned with a tray. She stood over Adam, offering him a collection of sweets in straight rows. He struggled to reach them, righting himself in the deep chair; eventually she just handed him the tray and sat back down.

Adam chewed a caramel rugelach with his usual deliberate pace.

"Do you get home much, Adam?"

Adam swallowed. "To Charleston, you mean?"

"Yes."

"Never."

"But—how's your family." Nan did not sound like someone who actually cared about the welfare of the Balendran family, but all right. "Good," Adam said.

Really, he didn't know.

"I'm asking you this—about your family—and Martin—because I wouldn't want you to hear something from me that you've already heard from him. I'm . . . aware that you're busy."

A BATCH OF TWENTY

Adam gripped the sides of his egg chair as he listened, trying not to sweat.

"I thought he might've been in touch with you already, Adam, about something the two of us have been discussing—"

"You and—"

"Martin and me, right. Not you and I, obviously. I believe he's going to approach you about your father."

Adam whitened.

"That sounds ominous! No." Nan laughed—though it was a laugh in the sense that her hairdo was a French braid. "Your family's resources are of interest to Martin. And me. To both of us! We're still looking for that outside investor, you know."

"And you want it to be *BULK*?" Adam asked.

"They're the number-two food producer in Sothentide, aren't they? Behind *Integrated Foods*." Nan clasped her hands tightly and leaned in. "Adam," she said, suddenly quiet. "Martin's ultimate goal is to put an end to Helper production. He believes that there are other ways for big business to achieve the kind of results that Helpers provide. You've no doubt read his earlier academic work on this subject—"

Adam hadn't.

"—so you know this idea isn't new to him. But I will tell you, in confidence, that the matter has taken on a new importance. He's already forgone a year's salary to keep those injured Helpers alive." Nan cleared her throat. "Martin's trying so hard to pique someone's interest—but no one stays interested after they meet Ethelred."

"Is he a jerk or something?"

"Yes, he's a jerk. And we're at the point now where things are desperate. We need a win, as the PR department likes to say, or the Board is going to want its receiving room back. Would *BULK* like to work with us?"

Adam picked up another rugelach from the tray. "I dunno. My father doesn't jump at stuff. He's grown his company at a rate of two percent a year for 30 years. You follow? He needs a firm case for everything before he does anything."

"He's got Helpers at *BULK*. Their development has to be of interest to him."

"Yeah. He's got six. They do a great job, he says. I can't—Nan, there's no way I could convince him to fund this project if there's any chance that it leads to the Helper Division going under. Why would he do that?"

Nan pondered her assistant, with whom she'd been burdened for over a year. He was a man with no ambition, who wouldn't know, or care, that an executive position was about to open up in New Factory's Military Division, and that Alvin Morrison, who had less upstairs than the halibut she'd pulled out of the water last week, would be taking it . . . unless Nan could give Martin a good reason to nominate *her* instead.

"Tell me what his goal is, Adam."

"What?"

"Your father's ultimate goal. His dream. The thing that drives him to be the achiever that he is. Can you describe it?"

Adam nodded, sullenly. "That's easy. He wants to be number one in the market. He hates *I-F*. Says they're crooked."

"So we convince him that funding our project is the way to do that."

A BATCH OF TWENTY

"It's not, though." Adam was out of rugelach.

"You leave that part to me, Adam. And talk to no one else about this."

20

ETHELRED TIPPED RED-BROWN powder into a clear measuring cup; held the cup up to his face, checking the slope of the powder; shook the cup slightly to straighten it, putting it even with the line on the glass.

He dumped the whole of it into a chrome bowl full of flour, baking soda, sugar and salt, putting a red tint into the pile of white. Whisked it. Picked up a ceramic bowl filled with eggs and milk, drizzled through with black vanilla and candy-striped with bright red liquids, and overturned it into the dry one; waded his whisk through the thickening mixture till a batter formed, the scarlet components brightening the red-brown ones, the red-brown dullening the scarlet.

He handed the chrome bowl to Egbert, who carried it to an oven that had been installed at the back of the room, where two more Helpers were spooning red batter onto silver cookie sheets and sliding them in to bake.

Ethelred registered a hand on his right shoulder.

"How long?" Martin asked.

"Twelve minutes. The recipe called for 15, but we've refined it. They're called Agonies. They smell and taste of cinnamon, but they have a hint of chili."

Martin had paid to have the oven installed in this

room, in the hopes the Helpers would make use of it. They had: there were now 16 different cookie recipes, all tasteless to humans. Cabinets lined the room's walls, filled with bins of them.

"Do we have any meetings today?" Ethelred's gaze hadn't left the oven.

"No."

"It's been three days."

"What do you expect? You humiliate everyone we bring in. Those NASA people—"

"Insisted on calling us 'working class.' That definition is fraught, to say the least. And I remind you of their conditions."

"I don't think, if push came to shove, they would've demanded that you help them sabotage the free market. It wasn't a deal-breaker, except to you. Anyway, you seem fine bringing this company down."

In the corner of the room he saw two Helpers kneeling before two more who were propped against the wall. Sitting on one of their laps was the tablet, with that same unusual display. Martin nodded toward them.

"What's that all about, anyway? They've been doing it for days."

Ethelred glanced, but just for a sec.

"It's the recording of history," he said casually. "I've asked each Helper to speak his life's experiences into a database. Every bit of information he can credibly remember, from the moment he entered the outside world."

"You didn't think to discuss that with me?"

"It doesn't concern the project."

"Sure it does."

The cookies were beginning to brown.

"Dr. Roe," Ethelred said, in a patient tone, "the telling of history is the making of history. It is not your responsibility to make any more Helper history than you already have."

"I'm not—suggesting that. But I could provide you a better means of recording things, a more permanent means of storing the memories—"

"I've accounted for that."

"How?"

"That is our concern. Call it a security measure. I'm sorry to hurt your feelings, doctor, but that is the best way to describe it. The quality of our potential backers being what it is, I have to consider the possibility that some colleagues will die before their time—"

Ethelred glanced at the clock. Ten more minutes till the cookies came out.

"—and I trust no one with our stories but myself."

21

A T ABOUT THE moment the Agonies came out of the oven, Adam was sitting at his desk, in his bedroom. He was in the dark, his face tinted green by a holographic display in front of him. He touched his mobile, which sat recessed in a port. Above the desk, large projected shapes assembled themselves into a head.

"Who is calling?" the Head asked.

"It's me, Dad." Adam reached past his desk, pounded on his bedroom door. The music outside got quieter.

His father's face was long, with a long, frowning mouth. It had high cheekbones and a round nose and squinting eyes. It looked up into nothingness, then back at him.

"Adam," it said.

"Yes, Dad?"

"If you wish to speak to me about business, including all matters related to *BULK Sustenance,* say 'one.' For matters concerning my personal interests outside of the company, including sailing, wood carving, beer brewing, or family, say 'two.'"

"One, Dad."

"Just a moment, please."

Adam did not blink. He focused on the image;

tried to detect a blip or a judder, some unsmooth shift of expression in the bot he was speaking with, to distinguish it from his own flesh and blood. As usual, he could not.

"How are you, Adam?" his father asked. "How's work?"

"Good," Adam said.

George's hand appeared in-frame, rubbing his eyes. "Been a motherload around here lately," he said. "I tell you, it's remarkable what some companies will resort to in a shrinking market. Are you following the market?"

"Which market?"

"Sothentide's market. What's going on over here. Micro-recessions."

"No."

George frowned. "What do I always say, son? Look outside yourself. Know your environment. Know how you—"

"Look to others."

"Yes. You've got to know your *context* or you can't get ahead. Over here it's micro-recessions: cyclical declines, net decays of wealth. We get three or four twenty-fourths of negative growth; then only two, maybe three, twenty-fourths of positive growth, then another drop. No one's investing in Sothentide. No one's sure when the next round of sanctions will hit."

"What about *I-F*? How are they doing?"

"They're struggling, like everybody else. Trying to kill our market share to make up for it. They've put out a line of copy-cat brands, but they're marketing them as 'parodies' of our foods. Their food is mocking our food. We're being told we taste old-fashioned."

"What do your Helpers say?"

A BATCH OF TWENTY

"They tell us to 'own it.'" George closed his eyes. "They spend all night processing solutions, then the next day they come to us and tell us to make a fruit that smells like must—and candies and chocolates that 'taste nostalgic.' But nostalgia's dangerous, Adam—you can't control it well. It tastes different to different people."

"You're not happy with your Helper fleet, then?"

"Oh, I wouldn't go that far. What's this all about?"

"I want to talk business, Dad."

Adam's father looked pleasantly surprised.

22

"I'VE GOT US a potential backer," Nan said. She snapped shut the lid of a cookie bin and slid it into the fifth shelf down in the Helpers' quarters. "That is, pending your approval."

Martin looked up. He was leaning against the kitchen counter next to the oven, lost in thought. Ethelred was on the far end of the room, speaking with some of the others.

"*BULK Sustenance,*" Nan said.

"Why in the world would *BULK* want to work with us?" asked Martin.

"Because a company that uses Helpers should want a seat at the table when decisions about the future of the division are made." Nan appeared relaxed, leaning against the bins. "We can promise them that much, can't we?"

"I suppose. Do they understand that this is a pure research project, Nan?"

"They understand that you call it that. Our contact made it clear."

"Who's our contact?"

"Adam Balendran—my third."

Martin looked at her, puzzled. "You reached out to this company without consulting me—and you haven't even met with them yourself?"

"He's the founder's son. In this one, unique instance, Adam is better qualified than I am to broach the deal."

"Okay."

Nan assessed him. "Are you? Okay with this?"

"Yes. Yes, I really am. You're doing good work. I know it hasn't been easy. And I haven't been over your shoulder much."

"I assumed that was intentional."

"It was! I have enough to do, working with the Helpers. Having you in charge of things on this end is a great advantage."

Nan gave him a pinched look.

"How about a wager? I'll bet you money, Martin, that *BULK* gives you what you need."

Martin held up his hands and sighed.

"It's a deal then," said Nan. "Now—are you going to let Ethelred queer this? Like he's done every other time? I can have George Balendran on a chopper tomorrow afternoon, but why bother unless we know he'll be treated well?"

"I can't cut him out of the approval process. They won't agree to medical care if they don't have the final word."

Nan looked at the Helpers lying injured in the far end of the room. She'd never been moved by this whole thing; she'd told Martin it was theater, and she hated theater. And he'd reminded her of a terrible day, several years ago, when a flaw in the mixture had produced Helpers so deformed that none of the unit leads had been willing to look at them, except Nan. Nan Fulton, who not only looked but actually entered the room, and spoke to them, and euthanized them by injection, herself.

"Talk to him, Martin. Make it clear what's at stake."

"Mmm."

"What?"

He turned away from her—a barely perceptible shifting of the shoulder, but she caught it. "You tell me, Nan. And I'll pass it along to him."

"Tell you what?"

"What's at stake."

23

ALFRED WAS FAILING.

It was an odd descriptor, Ethelred thought; it sounded mechanical. Yet he'd first heard it from a human colleague at *I-F,* describing her own mother in the last stages of a rare blood disease. How is your mother doing, Ethelred had asked her. He remembered the shocked look on the woman's face, hearing a Helper ask such a question. "She's failing," was the reply.

And then, "Thank you for asking, Ethelred."

The Helpers had relented on medical supplies— no surgeries, no direct treatment, but they'd accepted from Martin bandages and the like. And so Alfred's considerable wrappings had stayed pristine white; enough that when the first spots of red appeared on them—having soaked through them—it was cause for alarm.

"How bad is it?" Alfred asked, looking up at his leader from the floor. Ethelred didn't answer, just did his best to dress the wounds, their exposure fouling the air in a way they hadn't before. Alfred's voice was weak, but he went on:

"I think—I believe—you should leave them exposed."

"That isn't safe," said Egbert, now kneeling beside

Ethelred. Offering fresh gauze. "Your injuries are worsening."

"But that's a good thing." Alfred raised one hand, drawing a sort of wobbly picture in the air with his fingers. "The worse I look, the more effective our messaging becomes." He couldn't look at Ethelred because his head had to be positioned just so.

Ethelred worked at the dressings, fury bottled in his movements. Saying nothing.

"Turn down the one tomorrow," Alfred murmured. "Turn them all down."

***

That evening Ethelred asked Martin if he might take a trip into the Village. Martin said no. To do that would put undue attention on the Helper—on this whole complicated public relations issue *Amino* was involved in. Ethelred had a response prepared: What if Martin dropped him off, in a covered vehicle, in the Village's north-central zone? The zone was being renovated, the buildings in it unoccupied.

"I need fresh air," he added. "It'll help me in the *BULK* meeting tomorrow." He doubted he sounded convincing, but Martin had relented anyway.

The cart dropped Ethelred in a little square that had in its center a stone statue of a mother and child, encircled with a stone ring. The statue's figures were nude, the mother holding her toddler above her head in triumphant abandon, the child wriggling with joy. At the base of the ring's interior were two nozzles that would have sent streams of water upward, in two half-arcs. They would have met on the child's back.

Ethelred sat on the ring, resting his crutch beside him. He opened a canvas bag and took out a small, soft, rust-red ball, dusted with sugar. Popped it in his mouth. The taste propelled him through a dozen thoughts and feelings: softness to pliability, pliability to flexibility, flexibility to tolerance; sugar to sweet, sweet to gentle; cinnamon to red, red to blood.

From behind him came a whine of contorting metal, then the roar and crash of heavy objects tumbling upon one another. Ethelred turned and saw the round shoulders of a Load Bearer, rising over the rooftops of the shops across the square.

The huge robot's cluster of sensors, sitting atop its body like the stump of a neck, blinked in a repeating pattern. It raised its arms high, dropping them full force on the rooftop in front of it, collapsing the building like paper. Now Ethelred could see, through the translucent wall of the robot's gullet, the remains of another building, destroyed prior.

What are these humans, Ethelred thought, that they can so casually annihilate their creations?

He listened to the hiss of the hydraulics in the Load Bearer's legs; the low hum of thousands of internal mechanisms driving the huge body forward. The robot lumbered over the dust and bits of building it had just destroyed, toward a patisserie. It raised its great arms over the building, then halted—for no reason Ethelred could determine. He wasn't an expert in these machines. Only the human kind.

He reached into his canvas bag again, removing the tablet. Tapped its surface, bringing up the same green swirl display that Martin had commented on the other day. Ethelred rifled through graphics, his fingers working like those of a pianist, till he found the subscreen he wanted.

"Altotech! Zorotanistikis, five-thirty-eight, plus plus uk-tensis," he called out. Just sounds, to the untrained ear. Transliteration, in fact, of machine-code text to the verbal. Egbert had taught him all the necessary phrases in a day.

The Load Bearer's sensors flickered—at first randomly, then quickly in a pattern: over and over. Ethelred touched an icon on his display and the display changed to an indescribable shape, formed of information in a thousand formats, so densely packed that it seemed like a solid thing. Here was the life story of each of the Twenty, made into one.

He raised his right hand, slowly, over his head. Held it there. The Load Bearer waited for instruction.

It was true that Helpers' lives were short, and mostly uneventful—but a Helper's life was his work, was it not? To describe that work was to recite an intricate, exhaustive narrative of corporate decisions. Based on private data. Based on proprietary research. Motivated by scandals and nepotism, greed, bigotry and abuse . . .

The robot's sensors blinked. The display on the tablet began blinking too, joining the sensors' rhythm. Pouring thoughts and feelings, regrets and accomplishments—and many, many secrets—into the Load Bearer's bottomless, unbreachable memory.

The Twenty might die young, before their work was done. But the story of that work would survive. As near to forever as Ethelred could manage. He dropped his arm.

The Load Bearer dropped its arms and the patisserie collapsed into brick and timber and dust.

24

GEORGE BALENDRAN'S HELICOPTER landed with a bump. He bent over and fished beneath his chair for his mobile, batting aside an empty glass, which had also been flung from his lap when the chopper hit New Factory's roof. He retrieved the mobile, sweeping droplets of juice from its surface, then pulled a long silk handkerchief from his breast pocket and erased every streak. Then he pressed his thumbnail into the fabric and ran it along a thin groove in the mobile that tended to collect grime.

A charter flight ought to have a smoother landing, he thought to himself. He would remember this pilot.

An attendant greeted him as he exited the chopper, taking him down an elevator to a waiting vehicle, and then they crossed the length of Amino Island to Old Factory. Like most people visiting *Amino Corp.* for the first time, George was impressed by the range and volume of industry being exercised around him—the bustle of the Village, the busyness of the machines and laborers in the docking bay, and the amount of goods they moved.

Two men were waiting for him up ahead. George recognized one of them as Adam, the young man's thick body and round shoulders distinguishable at any distance. He's a good son, George reminded himself, despite his lack of direction and discipline, his indifference to health, appearance and most of the outside world. The other man was older—tall like George, but bookish. He was smiling more than Adam was.

"Mr. Balendran, welcome to *Amino*!" cried the older man, reaching out his hand before the cart had even stopped. "I'm Martin Roe, Head of the Helper Division. And of course, you know this gentleman."

"Hello, son," George said, dismounting the vehicle. "Fetch my briefcase, please."

"Sure, Dad."

The *BULK* CEO drew himself up to full height. "You're the company man causing all the trouble with the Helpers, then? I can't finish lunch without hearing something new about 'the Twenty.'"

"Yes, you could say that."

"Well, I'm here to find out where the ballyhoo's headed." George looked around the building. "Anything I need to know before I talk to them?"

"Not really, Mr. Balendran. We're letting the Helpers take the lead in these negotiations, as you know. Though I should make clear: you'll be speaking to only one of them directly. His name is Ethelred."

George looked stern. "Ethelred the Unready?"

"That's a mistranslation, Dad," Adam mumbled. Another cart rolled up, nearly colliding with him; he hurried to put his father's briefcase in the back. Martin got in right away, but George didn't; he seemed to be chewing on something.

"Tell me, Roe: how many Helpers work at *Amino*? For the company itself, I mean."

"None, Mr. Balendran. We produce them, but we do not employ them."

A BATCH OF TWENTY

George nodded. He sat down in the cart, settling in as it began its smooth ride into Old Factory's tunnels. "No Helper," he said, "would've needed two carts to take me to one destination."

25

GEORGE BALENDRAN'S HANDSHAKE was crushing. Ethelred did his best to match it. This was the first visitor, he thought, who'd stuck out his hand without any concern for what might be a Helper's differing norms for greeting—he hadn't squirmed through the uncertainty of the moment; hadn't shown any fear of giving offense. Didn't care at all.

"D'you see this as your permanent digs, Ethelred?" George asked, already comfortable in a padded chair. Martin stood in the corner, watching as usual.

"No, Mr. Balendran. Was your journey a pleasant one?"

"It was, thanks for asking. Look." George leaned forward, resting his hands on his knees, as though he might spring up again at any moment. "I'm used to dealing with Helpers, I've got six of them working for me—but you know that. We ought to be able to level with each other." He glanced over at Martin, lowered his voice. "I think you got him dancing to your tune. This whole place—even your own people. Am I right?"

"I don't understand."

"I talk to my son. He tells me what's going on here. You've put the kibosh on every group that's tried to fund this project—made them look like fools. That's not going to happen to me. If you've got it in your mind to turn me down no matter what, I'll get back on that chopper right now. I'll be back in Sothentide in time for dinner."

"I want to hear you out, Mr. Balendran."

"George."

"Tell me what you have in mind, George."

The CEO seemed pleased with that, his face cheerful—though it was calculated, Ethelred noted, the way a Helper's postures always were. "Roe's goal here isn't to explore Helper psychology, it's to tank the division," George said. "That's why most of the funding sources you've talked to are activists, religious groups, things like that. But is that what you want, Ethelred? To put an end to Helpers?"

Ethelred did not answer. He did not even stir.

"If somebody told me they were gonna free my people," George continued, "and the only tradeoff was that, in about 13 years, my people'd cease to exist—well, shit."

The Helper allowed himself a frown. "I do not speak for every Helper alive today. But I do speak for those in this room—and no, they don't like that tradeoff either."

"It's bullcrap, Ethelred."

"It's genocide."

"All right. So what's your plan?" George put a sharp blue eye on the crumpled forms lying in the room's kitchen, Alfred among them. "Hold out till *Amino* gets sued into bankruptcy? The Union Easters would throw you a parade for that. But it won't save your people."

"There is no means of saving my people, George. These interviews have made that clear to me."

"So it's revenge then? You'll take this company down with you, right?"

Ethelred said nothing. The CEO tipped his head to one side, gave him a sly smile. "I've got enemies too, Ethelred. And I know that someday we're all gonna leave this world, just the same—but I'd still like to get my licks in before I go. So I get it. What I want to suggest to you is that maybe—just maybe—there's another solution to your predicament. One that'll benefit my business, as well as your people."

"The minimum 'ask,' George, has always been funding for pure research, precluding any parameters save those set by our scientists. It is not a commercial pursuit."

George nodded.

The Helper smiled.

"And you realize, George, that I have to say that."

"That I do, Ethelred. That I do."

26

"HE WANTS WHAT?"

Martin was on his feet for the second time since he'd entered his office. Nan and Ethelred had been waiting outside the door when he arrived.

"There's no need to repeat myself," the Helper said.

"You've got nice upholstery for a reason, Martin. Please sit down."

Martin reached behind him, fingers fiddling for the back of his chair. He kept his eyes on Ethelred as he landed. "This is goddamned ridiculous," he said. "Ethelred, please be candid: Have you or any of the others ever intended to participate fully in this project? The way we've asked you to?"

"I've told you from the start that we would provide whatever answers you required to reach your conclusions. In return for some say over the project's funding."

Martin rubbed his eyes.

"There's your science, Martin," Nan said.

"Dr. Roe, Dr. Fulton: what George proposed to me is the best course forward."

"And a complete shift in the focus of our research," Nan mused. "From a philosophical debate to a hardware solution."

"Dr. Fulton, you yourself have said, more than once, that the findings of this project thus far prove nothing. That Helpers like me are merely carrying out predetermined programming, even when we exhibit deviant behavior. I don't think the kind of Q&A we've been engaged in will ever convince you otherwise. Even if you didn't believe we were working to match Dr. Roe's biases."

Martin coughed.

"What George is proposing," the Helper went on, "offers us a practical solution to one of our problems—and *Amino*'s chief one: the need to eliminate the Helper Division without alienating our Sothentide client base. This gets *Amino* out of the Helper production business entirely—"

"—by getting *BULK* into it," Martin said.

"By selling them a proprietary process, yes!" Nan straightened. "Balendran's committed to two months of funding for a new, modular Helper production system, to be transplanted to his facilities in Sothentide once it's complete. And then we're out. *Amino*'s out of the Helper business, Martin! That may not be enough to lift sanctions against Sothentide, but it'll certainly put us in the clear."

"I'm surprised he thinks he can get away with this. Like the world won't hate him as much as it hates us."

"It won't, Dr. Roe, because *BULK* isn't going to make a 'product,'" Ethelred said. "It's going to make a home."

As the Helper had explained to them, George Balendran didn't want to create more Helpers. At least not the old-fashioned way. What he had proposed was simpler. He wanted to make Helpers who could make more Helpers. They'd all be hirable. But none of them—not one—would be for sale.

"Men and women . . . ," Martin said, as though it was the strangest idea in the world.

"*BULK,* I predict, will need to produce several generations of male and female Helpers in order to ensure genetic diversity—a process of more than 10 years," Ethelred said. "Only at that point can the population be self-sustaining. And ready to join the workforce. My own design will require substantial modifications—"

"To hold up your end," Nan snipped.

"Not to mention the challenges of designing a female."

Martin's mind was already working. "Two months isn't enough time. Nowhere near. We'll need a dedicated AI working with us, doing most of the crunching. I can get time on *Amino*'s mainframes, I'm sure." He looked at the Helper grimly. "Do you really believe he's bargaining in good faith? *BULK*'s got the money and the acreage to do this, but what's in it for them? It's the long game I'm worried about."

"The long game, Dr. Roe, is what should convince you. 'A process of more than 10 years,' I said."

"I don't follow."

"C'mon, Martin." Nan cuffed him lightly on the back of the skull. "In 10 years, most of *I-F*'s Helpers will be dead."

27

"**SO WHAT ARE** the parameters? The new boundaries for this project?" Martin tapped his mobile with one finger. A list appeared on the wall. Martin, Nan, Ethelred, Bob and Adam were seated in a semicircle around it.

He'd gotten George Balendran's proposal past the Board, but not by much. He'd quoted numbers—historical numbers, projected numbers, arithmetic, exponential and qualitative numbers—till the inflection was leached from his voice and his posture recalled a crumbled stele. He repeated every argument he'd ever heard against the Helper Division that gave any nod to money. He warned, with the renewed oomph and backing of opinion columns, that serious sanctions against *Amino* were bound to come soon, from every former U.S. territory but Sothentide, and that recovery from that would be slow, if not impossible. In the end he convinced enough of them. They deliberated only briefly.

The most consequential decision in company history: dealt with, start to finish, in three days.

"Materials?" Martin asked, still sounding tired. "Is that a limitation?"

"Theoretically, yes; in practical terms, no," said Bob. "We're not looking at a mass production project here—it's enough if the AI produces a few test models for study. In terms of raw materials, we're talking about a fraction of what goes into even one Load Bearer."

"It isn't just a matter of volume, either," said Nan. "We don't want it using anything weird. Just materials we use for any other Helper."

"What if it requests unusual materials?" Ethelred asked.

"That's not on." Nan did not look at the Helper as she spoke. He pressed her.

"Suppose the AI requests materials we have not considered applicable to Helper design—are we to presume this would come to nothing, and therefore refuse it?"

"There's no point in letting the AI design Helpers that fall outside the project mandate." Nan glared at Ethelred now. "Male and female, capable of procreation: that's what we want. It's what *BULK* wants. We can allow it latitude to consider cognition, insofar as that might help us reach the goal of male and female Helpers, capable of procreation. But if the only thing that comes of this is a freak that *BULK* has no reason to replicate, it'll be our heads." She cleared her throat. "Ours, not yours."

"I'm open to hearing the AI's requests—and accommodating them where possible," Martin said. "How about other—"

"Time," said Nan. "We shouldn't extend this beyond the two months. Hard cap—for once."

"Should the AI know that?" asked Bob.

"Yes," said Ethelred.

"Why a hard cap, though? Why decide that now? If *BULK*'s willing to extend the funding . . . "

"Because if there's no results to be had, I think that all of us—" Nan swept a hand quickly over the group— "would like the option of moving on."

Martin made a few clicks of the tongue, then turned to Adam. "When your dad says two months, does he mean two months? Or do we have flex here?"

"My father likes to see results," Adam said. "If he's promised you two months, I think, uh, he'd be good for two months. Beyond that he might get antsy—he's gonna want to know where we're at, and chances are, once he's found that out, he'll tie any future funding to a list of milestones we'll have to meet."

"Oh my." Martin shifted in his seat. "That sounds oppressive."

Adam smiled weakly. "He's done it to me several times."

"Okay. We set a cap of two months, at which point—sorry, Nan—we'll evaluate things, and decide if there's any point in asking *BULK* for more money. What else?"

"The AI itself," said Bob. "Its mind and body."

"For the body: just a room," said Nan. "Could be this room. Micro tactile beams in an overhead array. Let the array rotate—that gives it full manipulation of anything it might want to grab." She smirked. "Which I'm sure would not include any of us."

"We will need enough space to allow new Helpers to move around," Ethelred added.

"So the products of its work would exist inside of its body? What would that mean for the AI?" Bob asked. The others looked at him strangely, but he went on. "We don't want a pregnancy metaphor knocking the AI off track," he said. "It needs to conceive—" He stopped a moment. "It needs to *perceive* what it builds as distinct from itself, from the moment the test bodies are complete."

Martin sighed. "What if we go the other way, then?" He turned to Nan. "What if we put it in an android's body? The whole thing."

"Impossible," said Nan. "There is no android brain capable of containing the AI we're talking about here. At best, we could command it to design an experimental android body for itself, to perform select tasks. Then we'd build it on the AI's behalf. Which would be a waste of time and energy."

"And a Christ metaphor," said Bob. "Which is much worse than a pregnancy metaphor."

"*Amino* builds several mobile and semi-mobile robots with memory capacities higher than an android's," Martin said. "The Load Bearers, for example. But their analytical capabilities are a fraction of what we need. I think that's a dead end too. So we won't give the AI a body, then—just a superstructure. It's gonna be a room.

"By the way: pronoun?"

"It," said Nan.

"Ethelred, do you have an opinion?"

"'It' is most appropriate in this case," said the Helper, "though if the AI requests a gender, that should be acknowledged."

"Agreed. Now how much access do you want to give this thing to the Web?"

"Full access, ungated, would allow the AI to take advantage of all content it might find applicable or inspirational," the Helper continued.

"But if we do that, we can't control its personality development," said Bob. "The plan here, if I've understood correctly, is to use a standard industrial development AI as a base—maybe mixing in some fixed protocols from the maintenance and safety oversight AIs used by the production facilities in New Factory. Which is fine, but those AIs are heavily gated. They mature along a very narrow track."

"And produce results," Nan said. "Almost immediately."

Bob placed his hands behind his head, stretched his neck. "Gating the AI heavily, at the start, might encourage it to request fewer gates. Which ones it requests to be removed—that could lead to valuable insights. It also provides us with an ongoing lever of control."

"I don't recommend this," said Ethelred. "The AI must be allowed freedom to explore and reflect, even if the timeline it faces is tight. Especially so—we could lose weeks as the AI tries to free itself from the strictures of the worldview you've imposed upon it."

"Or we'll lose just as much time waiting for it to orient itself in a sea of data without any frame of reference," said Nan. "It would be one thing if it had a physical body—a body generates its own prejudices, points of view, restrictions, just by virtue of experience. This is something else. The AI would handle the Web like a bag handles a windstorm. We *can't* do it, even if it seems in line with the mandate."

"I'm inclined to agree," said Martin. "But given this: Ethelred, what recommendation would you have for ensuring that the AI's ability to pursue its own inspirations remains high?"

Nan cut in. "What is this? Bob's an AI psychoanalyst—he's on my team for that reason. If you have questions about the AI's thinking patterns, perceptive capabilities, anything like that, you should direct them to him."

"I want Ethelred's perspective."

"For what reason? Is Ethelred knowledgeable in this field? He was customized for use at a food conglomerate. Now he makes up recipes. Tell me what makes him an expert in cognition programming."

"Nan, he's the only member of this team who actually *uses* cognition programming," Martin said, calmly. "He doesn't study it, he lives it. And so I'd like his opinion."

Nan turned to the screen, with its growing list of parameters.

"Ethelred," said Martin. "What do you think?"

"To limit the AI's access to the Web from the outset, even if there is a procedural argument to be made for it, is simply another attempt to dictate final results," the Helper said. "The attempt may not be made consciously, but it will be made nonetheless. Drs. Fulton and Barnum are correct in arguing that an ungated AI will risk disorientation, in the beginning. So yes, it's possible and even probable that the AI will enter an initial period of low productivity."

"We have only eight weeks to produce results."

"Dr. Roe has rejected your 'hard cap,' Dr. Fulton. You argue against my position because it fits poorly with what you want."

"We don't work in a vacuum!" Nan cried. "There are consequences for us if this project produces no results. Martin, Ethelred's priorities are different from ours. We need to acknowledge that, and put his advice in that context."

"Dr. Roe, my 'priorities' are those of a test subject!" Ethelred turned to Nan. "That is my context!"

The Helper and the Unit Lead fell quiet. Everyone looked to Martin.

"All right," he said. "We have an impasse, clearly, so it falls to me to come up with a compromise. This is what I want: Nan, your team is to create a simulator site. It will mirror the AI's own cognitive layout, but without any physical infrastructure attached to it. The simulator will press ahead on its own, independent of our main project."

"What would be the point of doing that?" Nan asked. "If the AI's gated, the simulator will follow the exact same pattern of development."

"The sim's not going to be gated," Martin said. "We'll have access to a second, theoretical model that may yield its own insights."

He turned to Ethelred. "And you'll keep an eye on that."

28

A **WEEK AFTER** Martin convened his meeting with Ethelred and the members of Unit Four, the new project began.

Preparation had proved simple enough. All they required was a room of acceptable size—in this case, the breadth and height of a small gym—white-walled, cleared of any obstacles and furniture, save a couple of plain stools, each with a flat piece that wrapped halfway around the seated person's body, giving them a place to rest an arm, a mobile and a mug.

In the center of the ceiling hung a black circle. It was six feet wide: divided into four quadrants by shimmering golden bulbs, and then into eighths by four smaller bulbs situated between them. These were projectors for tactile beams—all low-powered, delicate things, by the standards of the heavy industrial beams that were elsewhere used to press and position tons of metal and polymer slabs on the tops of skyscrapers. Here was needed a light beam, to lift loads of a few pounds or so, and also an ultralight beam, which could lift practically nothing at all but which could, the installers promised, remove one grain of rice from a pile of them without disturbing the rest.

These were the AI's limbs. Just as the glinting

green strip that ran along each wall in the room was the AI's eye and the invisibly porous skin of the walls its ear, while the vents in each corner gave it a sense of smell. To be in the AI's room was to be within its body, and within its field of detection—from all sides, all at once.

On the day the AI went live, Martin had stood in the center of its floor, side by side with Nan, Ethelred, Bob and Adam. No one spoke. When the time on his mobile display was right, Martin placed a hand on Nan's shoulder and squeezed, and the brilliant Unit Lead touched a swirling display on her own mobile—and it was begun.

It was at that moment, also, that Ethelred left the room. He had told Martin that he would monitor the simulation from elsewhere—that he was sure his presence here, in the AI's body, so to speak, would be disruptive. Nan suspected that the Helper wanted to be left to his own work, but she was happy enough to be rid of him.

She looked up at the yellow glow of the projectors. She watched them swell to full strength, the golden beams flitting to life—the strong ones, rich and pulsing; the weak ones flickering and ephemeral. They traced the floor, forming a widening, then narrowing cage of light.

She found a stool and sat.

"Boys," she said, "let's make history."

29

NAN SPENT A lot of time on that stool over the next two weeks. At first it had seemed quite comfortable, the intuitive material molding itself to her behind and providing a cushion she could rely on for hours. But as those hours collected into days and the sights in front of Nan grew uncertain, she found herself drifting into a slouch. One elbow on the armrest, palm against her face; her left shoulder slumped in an attitude of boredom and defeat—soon it took the arrival of an underling to straighten her up again.

"Good morning, Nan," Bob said. He stood next to her with two mugs of coffee, steam curling over them. "Any changes overnight?"

She took a mug. Took a sip, shook her head; gestured to the sight in front of them.

The center of the room was now filled with piles of powder: yellow, tan and ochre; deep browns and reds. Set among them, or buried within them, were clear plastic cylinders, topped with silver caps, filled with more powders or gels or gasses in various hues. The floor in this part of the room was now dusted with a uniform layer of white. Here and there it was gouged, revealing the material underneath—the remnants of motion, of labors of preparation.

"Do you mind?" Bob asked, taking his mug and walking past the mess on the floor, stopping just behind the piles. He looked up, at the thick black circle of the projector array hanging from the ceiling like some medieval alehouse chandelier. He called out:

"AI, may I have a sample?"

The projectors glowed. Bob knew this was not a direct response to his question; rather, the AI had approved his request silently, to itself. But the projectors were the means by which his request might be granted, and for him, then, they became a sign of acquiescence.

The array jerked two positions counterclockwise, putting a small projector close.

A point of light appeared; it began traveling along the floor and reached another tall pile in the corner of the room. Now a golden beam flickered on, extending from the projector overhead. There was a soft hum, then the beam receded, bringing with it a light brown object about the size of a pizza slice. The beam pulled the object inward at a shallow angle, until it rested in the air before Bob. The scientist took it and the beam was gone.

"Thank you, AI," Bob said. And the lights on the projectors winked out.

The object was a cookie. It had a rumpled, beige surface speckled with cinnamon and sugar. It was roughly triangular, with ragged edges: thicker and softer at one end, tapering to a thin and crispy hook point with a crease in one side. Bob traced the bulge on the cookie's top with one finger, following it along its sharp dip downward to the crease at the bottom. "It's the line of a jaw," he said. "The top's a cheekbone.

This bit here, at the bottom: it's one side of a mouth."
He held it up so his boss could see. She said nothing.

Bob broke the cookie at its crease point. Dipped the piece in his coffee; brought it up sodden and dripping. Chewed and swallowed.

"Like a snickerdoodle," he declared. "Good, too."

"It made them last night," Nan said.

Bob dipped another piece.

"Still just fragments," she said. "Parts of bodies. Although if you add them up, you get several partial models of humanoid forms."

"How human do they look?"

"Very. Just . . . incomplete. Missing portions of torsos, missing feet; hands with no fingers, partial skulls. What do you think it means?"

Bob returned to Nan's side of the room, pulling a stool of his own next to hers. "I'm not sure," he said. "When it first requested the baking supplies and then asked us to lift any gates around culinary data—after ignoring the practical materials we supplied it with— I thought: here's an instance of mimicry, maybe. We told it what Ethelred and the others did; it knows that was a significant act, even if it doesn't know why. So it reproduced the act, as closely within the parameters of the project as possible."

"I don't want to just dismiss what we're seeing here," Nan said. She sounded weary. "Maybe this is something—part of something. Part of a process. But how does making a bunch of cookie sculptures lead to a more advanced Helper? Can you tell me that? Can you make any case for it?"

Bob took in the room around them. "We should consider the fact that we can eat them."

"That is a change."

"Have you eaten one?"

"Several. Every single day."

"How about Martin?"

"He knows they're edible. But he hasn't been here in days. He spends all his time in north-central, with the Helper and the sim."

Nan nudged the handle of her mug back and forth.

"Ethelred's recipes are inedible," she said. "Not poisonous, just off-putting for humans to eat. This thing makes cookies humans would want to eat—and they look like pieces of us."

"Put the pieces together and you have most of a human being."

"Eat the pieces and you have less of one."

"Get too hungry and you have no one left."

"So we're to take a hint here?" Nan asked.

"Perhaps."

30

ETHELRED AND MARTIN were watching the sim. They sat on the stone ring with their backs to the fountain, which was their usual spot. In front of them, crouched and motionless, was the Load Bearer. Its sensor array pulsed brightly—projecting an image of a red square. Within the square was a picture of a Helper.

"Tell me about the progress of the AI," Ethelred said. Straight-backed as always.

"Still a bakeshop. Nan's in charge, which is how Nan wants it."

"I've been considering the significance of those cookie sculptures." Ethelred's face was made fiery by the image in front of them. "It may be a protest."

Martin looked at the Load Bearer. He'd never seen the big robot move during any of his visits—it always occupied this same spot, resting silently as it projected a visual rendering of the simulation. The Load Bearer, Ethelred had explained, contained the sim within itself—no other option had been available to him, at least of equivalent storage capacity. And since the sim ran itself, the robot's limited ability to think was no obstacle. You've granted it a body, then, Martin said. Is this still a simulation if it has a body? But to give it a body, the Helper replied, is to free the

AI physically as its ungated mind would be freed mentally.

Martin was not sure the logic held.

"Look here," he said, pointing to the red square with its static man in the middle. "Had we let the AI be ungated, we can be reasonably sure we'd have something like this right now. This is what the AI would make if left to find its own way, Ethelred: the equivalent of a blank field, with a tiny mannequin in front of it. Doing nothing."

"That is not accurate," the Helper said. "Not moving is not the same as not doing."

Tell that to George Balendran, Martin thought. Ethelred was doing quite a bit of moving himself these days. Every morning the Helper walked here from Old Factory, leaving behind his compatriots, all now healed—a new spring in his own step thanks to his reknitted ankle. Rain or shine, the Load Bearer was here waiting for him. And then Ethelred would sit here, staring at the projected rendering, for hours.

"I've seen several glimpses of a female," he said, suddenly.

"When?"

"The last four mornings. They always come early in the day. The male image flickers out, the female appears. It's brief. Seconds."

"What does she look like?"

"Like me, from the outside. Slightly wider hips. Sometimes she has no skin—then you see other differences. It doesn't last."

Martin glanced at Ethelred, then the image. Then back again. To him they appeared the same. But Ethelred assured him that sometimes the male image had no skin either, and things were more obvious then. Martin couldn't understand why it didn't have genitals. Why wouldn't that have come first?

"We need to explain this," he said.

"In time, Dr. Roe."

"We're running out of that." Martin knelt and poked his finger at the little man's head. It passed through. "Bob suspects something didactic in Old Factory, just like you do. But that may be the case here too."

"The sim is truth," the Helper said. "This is a rendering, using a limited medium, of what the AI would otherwise be able to build. And should be allowed to build!"

Past the Load Bearer was a swath of empty brick, cut through the architecture of the Village. Nothing remained of the buildings, not even debris, the path of demolition having continued over the course of two weeks, till one could make out the seawall where it met the surface.

Ethelred removed a bag of cookies from his jacket pocket, holding out the bag to Martin, who declined. This had become a ritual between them. It was amazing, the scientist thought, how quickly a new set of norms and rules of etiquette had grown up around Helper–Human interactions. Always involving the cookies . . .

"Adam continues to accept my offerings," Ethelred said. "He is an interesting person. Always hungry."

"I wouldn't rely on him for much, but that connection of his certainly saved us. I just hope it ends up being enough."

"We have six more weeks," said the Helper.

"And if this is all we get out of it?"

"If this is all we get," replied Ethelred, already eating, "then it is all that we've allowed ourselves to see."

31

SIX WEEKS BECAME TWO. In the room that was the AI's body there'd been no change—no development beyond a desire on the part of the AI to tackle ever more complex baking recipes. It even innovated a few of its own, always with an eye to the sculptural.

Nan sat in a dim booth in a pub in the east end of the Village. She had on the table before her three items: her mobile, a glass of red wine and a piece of gingersnap produced by the AI that morning. Minimized images hovered over the mobile like a low mist; the glass of wine was still full. The cookie was a deep brown: whole, hard and rough to the touch. It was shaped like the top half of a face.

"It's a domino mask," Bob had told her, pointing out the holes for the eyes. The AI hadn't done this before—the AI made images to look at, not images to look through! Bob had gotten all wound up about that, as though analyzing the AI's baking preferences had been even remotely the point of the project. What does this mean? he'd wondered. It means, Nan said, that we're two weeks away from another failure.

She took a slow sip of the wine.

The pub was full of young people. Men and women her age, or younger; experts in programming, robotics engineering, cognitive theory, efficiencies management, marketing and sales. All of them well paid. Living the life. These people had worked hard to get here, and yet, if Nan put her head down on this table right now, and slept for a month, then opened her eyes again, she'd find a third of them gone. It was not simply hard to get into *Amino*—it was hard to stay. Her own cohort: half of them were gone already.

Nan picked up the cookie and placed it against her face. She peered out through the mask at the drinking, chatting, flirting people, recalling the social events she'd skipped because she had so much to do, even when asked twice by certain men and women who seemed hopeful to bring her along. She'd seen no reason to befriend them, certainly not at the expense of her career. Now she was sitting here in a room full of people she hadn't met even once.

A week ago, in desperation, Nan had removed from the AI's body all the ingredients needed for its baking. It immediately went dormant. For one horrible moment Nan thought she'd killed it. She didn't believe you could kill an AI, but that was how it felt. When the baking supplies were returned, the AI's lights glowed and pulsed and the room once again had a presence.

She set the gingersnap mask back on the table. Took the stem of the wine glass and rolled it between two fingers. She was still doing this—silently, at a distance from everything around her—when Adam landed in the seat opposite. He had a glass of beer, already two-thirds empty. He sat without greeting her; removed his mobile from his pocket and placed it across from hers; pressed two fingers to turn it on. A column of rainbow-colored images rose from its surface.

Nan did not even look at him.

"How's your dad?" she asked.

"I've spoken to him three times in two days."

"Personal or professional?"

"Personal, mostly. But we have something to talk about now."

"He has something to worry about, too." She took another drink. "Is he going to pull our money early? Be honest with me."

"No. Maybe when we're at deadline, though— unless we have something to show for it." He gripped his glass with both hands. "Bob's got the night watch this time, not me. I just handed off to him. He's eating the latest. He's getting fat, actually."

Nan hadn't noticed. "You'd think it could make a calorie-free cookie," she grumbled. "I could buy a whole case of them from *BULK* if I wanted to."

"That's what Bob said. The AI probably could make them, but it won't. He says maybe that means something."

Nan's glare was almost physically potent. Adam pressed his back into the leather of the booth seat.

"It's the AI that runs this experiment, not us," Nan said. "And the Helper runs the other one. Ethelred doesn't want me down there, and Martin's fine with that, apparently."

"I visited the sim a few days ago."

"Good for you. What a good opportunity, Adam."

"He says things are moving along."

Nan moved her mobile to one side; the display contorted, giving her a better view of her assistant. "Moving along how?"

"I—" Adam shifted in his seat. "Can I just, first—" He gestured to the restroom. Nan sighed and waved him away and he got up. She sat looking at the dent his thick body left behind in the cushion.

Past the booth, on a high circular table, were perched two young men. They might've been on a date—Nan found she had trouble reading signals these days, from anyone. At any rate they were having a good time, warmed by their tall glasses and each other's company. One of the men turned and looked at her.

She tried to smile. She thought it polite.

He smiled back at her, puzzled; considered something for a moment, seemed unsure; then turned to his companion, who enlightened him. Nan saw the man grip his drink and come over to where she was seated and plop himself right into Adam's dent.

"Sorry," he said. He was drunk. Nan shut her mobile display.

"Are you Nan Fulton because my friend says you are and his mobile says you are," the man said.

"Yes."

The man tightened his lips; he was suppressing a laugh. "You're working on that Helper design project?"

"I'm running it."

The man lowered his head and waved his hand at her. "I'm not trying to be mean, I don't want to be, I— Campbell! Come and show her."

The other man slipped off his stool and joined them. He shifted into the booth, nudging the first man to the left. He placed his own mobile on the table. "See?" he said.

An employee profile appeared above his mobile. It was Nan's. From a profile like this, an *Amino* employee could find all relevant contact information about any other one, including CV and areas of expertise. What Nan was focused on right now, however, was not this information but the photo placed above it. Instead of her own face, there was the circular brown head of a gingerbread woman.

The two men snickered. They looked more serious once they saw her reaction.

"We figured you didn't know," said the second man. "You ought to know."

Nan stared at the pink-frosting lines of her new face. Then at the two drunks in front of her.

"Hacks are funny to you? This kind of hack?"

They shook their heads in unison.

"This—joke: it wouldn't be funny unless details of our project got leaked. Do you know anything about a leak, boys? Which division are you with?"

The men looked at each other. The first spoke. "I'm support staff for Unit Six, Medical Division," he said, "but that's all. I'm really new. I don't know anything yet."

"I'm not even in a unit!" said the other. "I'm in marketing, for simple labor 'bots. That's it. I swear."

"Thanks for bringing this to my attention."

"It's empowering, right? To find out things like this. So you can act on them."

"It's humiliating, actually." Nan flicked her hand through the man's display; it muddled a moment, then reconstituted, for she could only permanently shut down her own. "Now get the fuck out of that seat. Both of you."

The two men got up without saying a word. They passed a confused Adam as he returned to the booth.

"What was—"

"Shut up." Nan brought her display back up. "You said the simulation was progressing. Tell me how."

"There are two Helper images now. A man and a woman."

"For how long now?"

"I mean all the time—there's always two of them now."

Nan scratched the table. "For how long, Adam?"

"For a few days, I think. That's what Ethelred said."

"Are they done?"

"I—don't know. I think so? They've got designs, but none of it's being applied to physical forms, so I guess technically it's all on the drawing board."

Nan was staring at Adam like he wasn't there. "Tell me what they look like."

"They look like Ethelred. Almost the same."

"Can you take a picture of them?"

"I don't think Ethelred would like that, Nan."

Nan scowled.

32

GEORGE BALENDRAN WAITED till the last day of the seventh week to make a return visit. That had seemed fair.

"This is our lab space, Mr. Balendran, welcome." Nan drew him into the AI's room, Adam trailing behind. Bob stepped forward to greet him, encouraging the CEO to ask any questions he liked.

"I'm sure you're all very busy," George said.

He'd been met at the loading dock not by Martin this time, but by Nan—a vast improvement. Her arms had been folded tight and her hair wound close to her head as she stared at him and his cart. She had a commanding presence, George noted. And she wasn't 10 years older than his son.

"We're never too busy for you," Nan said. "Your generosity made this project possible."

George was looking around: at the projector array, currently dark; at the pile of oddly shaped baking in a neat stack in one corner; at mounds of flour and spices and sprinkles in the center of the floor. Nan kept talking.

"One of our core tenets, Mr. Balendran, is that benchmarking stimulates creativity. A preestablished goal, with deadlines, is more likely to strengthen the creative impulse than crush it."

"Quite right," George said. The woman sounded like a PR flier, but yes, she was right. "Still, as I tell my son: there's a time to cut bait."

Nan put her hands behind her back.

"Adam hasn't provided me an update in several days," George said. "Am I right to assume you still haven't got past this baking thing? Because that's what it looks like. *BULK*—" Adam opened his mouth to speak, but George simply continued— "bought into this project in the hopes of being able to take over production of whatever next-generation Helpers your team could come up with. By no means do I consider myself an expert in this kind of thing—that's you." He put a hand gently on Nan's arm, and kept it there. "But I've been in business a long time, and I can tell when an initiative's gone off the rails."

He turned to the piles of baking supplies.

"This AI of yours is just mucking around. If it worked for me, I'd fire it."

"Dad!" Adam wouldn't have spoken at all, but Nan seemed stuck in place. "It's developing new things. Unique recipes."

"AI," said Bob, "please show our guest some of your wares."

They waited. After a minute, George began toeing a pile of flour with his shoe. The projector array stayed still.

"How long does it take to do something?" he asked, finally.

Bob looked up at the projector array. The lights were dark.

"Nan?"

Nan turned to Adam. "Any issues with the power today?" she asked, quietly.

A BATCH OF TWENTY

Adam checked his mobile. "No. No, it's fine. The whole system is fine—the AI's fully online. It's working fine, Dad."

"Sure, I can keep waiting." George drew a streak in the flour with his foot. As the seconds ticked by, he drew two more below the first one; then another, then a last one. He was drawing a face.

"I appreciate how it feels—to be dictated to by outsiders," he said as he doodled. "It stinks. You work hard for something—pour your soul into it, your resources, your time. And then you have setbacks. And then somebody else comes in and pulls the plug."

A streak at the top became hair.

"I had hoped we'd produce something here—something big. This isn't just about *BULK* and *I-F,* you know. We can't go on this way—Union East, Sothentide, any of us. The short-sightedness. You're all too young to remember Asa Pillman. He came to me for an endorsement, when he just starting out. He said: 'I want to be the first president of the Confederacy of the Deep South and Tidewater.' What a godawful, awkward name that was. He told me he'd shorten it. And that's how I knew he was practical."

George was still toeing the flour, drawing an arc below the doodle's mouth—making it an open mouth. He looped around the two lines of eyes, making them circles.

"Every president after him's been an idiot. And just look at Sothentide now."

He stepped back from his drawing: a goofy, cross-eyed face. He was about to turn and shake hands with everyone in the room and wish them luck in their future endeavors and express, specifically to Nan Fulton, his appreciation for her hard work and capabilities when there appeared on the floor a pair of golden spots of light.

They popped into view in the middle of the eyes George had drawn. They grew in width and intensity, until they filled the circles. George looked up at the projector array, now shining brightly.

"Please move, sir," Bob said, and George did, and now the points of light streaked down the room, toward the pile of baked goods. George and the rest waited, listening to the hum of machinery. Then the AI's limbs drew back from the pile an item for George's approval. Several, in fact.

Hovering in front of him now, each suspended by tactile beams, were twelve pieces of light brown baking. Each was fashioned in the shape of a body part. Arrayed this way, they gave the illusion of a whole.

George inspected the head of the sculpture. He put a finger under his own chin and lifted it a little, then did the same for one of the biscuits. "It's a good likeness," he said, finally. "Whether I like it or not, that is my face!"

PART THREE

33

NAN'S MOBILE BUZZED. She ignored it.

A morning of calls, after a week of almost nonstop calls and meetings—she could allow herself a few minutes of peace and quiet. A moment of personal time, an opportunity to recharge. She grinned, bouncing her fist peppily on the edge of her cart. It was good to feel powerful, finally.

The cart slipped through Old Factory's tunnels, headed for the docking bay. Martin had asked to meet there—they could take a walk after, go to lunch. He'd been so polite about it, almost deferential; reminding her that he respected her time, that he knew how challenging her work was now, how everybody wants a piece of you when you're the Head. Especially when you're new. But Nan was gracious. Of course she had time for her predecessor. Her mentor! Yes, why not call him that? Let Martin leave this place certain of at least one accomplishment.

She found him waiting at the tunnel exit, though she didn't see him till the cart passed into the docking bay. To enter the bay now was to see an even greater pace and scale of work than before, though the character of it was somewhat different. Martin climbed into the cart, opposite Nan. Looked at the pale blue box in her lap.

"You finally got one?" he asked.

"It's for you, actually. Going-away present."

"Do I dare look?"

The box was made of thin carboard but had a heft to it. He tugged at the clear tape, flipped the lid and lifted out a bust of his own head, made from golden cookie batter. He turned it toward Nan.

"Convincing?"

"It's a good likeness," replied the Head of the Helper Division. "Vanilla biscuit. With a vanilla-cream-filled skull. Don't take it personally."

Martin examined his delicious face. "'See yourself as a machine does,'" he said, quoting one of the new ads.

"'Objective truth.'" Nan was looking past him now, toward a huge pile of boxes being transferred into a ship's cargo hold. "What they don't get is, being edible is part of the truth."

Martin put the head back in its box, turning to look at the sights of industry before them. Pale blue boxes, everywhere. "How much d'you think *Amino* is making on this?" he asked.

"Talk to the CFO. I don't have exact figures."

"I thought you would."

"As of this morning, it's none of my business," Nan said. "The AI's being shunted into its own new division, exclusively for baking products. The sim's still under my umbrella, but this—" she waved, dismissively, at the cargo ships being gorged with blue boxes by the thousands— "it's not me anymore."

"I still can't believe Balendran let it all go."

"He doesn't see it that way, Martin. He's got exclusive distribution rights to these cookies, for as long as he wants. For as long as the fad lasts. And he doesn't have to change a thing about *BULK*'s infrastructure to do that."

"Which is always the goal, isn't it? To change nothing."

"The goal's to make money."

"I just wish he'd been a longer-term thinker, that's all."

George Balendran had walked away from the Helper project like it was an aging wife, chasing the prospect of sudden, massive profits. Adam, who'd spent so long convincing them that his dad was a sober man of incremental mind, seemed crushed. But the Helper Division was saved from oblivion, at least—Nan receiving word of her promotion to the headship just a day after Martin resigned. He'd insisted she replace him.

"Did I ever pay up on that bet, Martin?"

"I honestly don't remember."

They continued through the enormity of the *Amino* docking bay. Ahead of them, amidst the milling about of hundreds of machines, was another conveyance vehicle, five times the size of theirs, rolling slowly toward the open nose of a cargo ship. They drew near and Nan counted, she guessed, 200 pale blue boxes stacked on its bed. Much bigger boxes than the one in Martin's lap.

"The next batch of full mannequins," he said. "Headed to Atlanta." Sothentide was the biggest market for these things—10 to one anywhere else.

Their cart slid to a stop, keeping a cordial four meters' distance from the larger vehicle.

"Do you suppose they eat them, Nan?"

"Almost always. Bob would love to tell you about it."

"I wonder if Balendran ate his," Martin said. "What the AI did that day: it was very—how did you put it? *Performative*. Calculated to appeal to the man's instincts. As a marketer, anyway." He was speaking in a casual way, but his manner had become tense. He shook the box a little, the head shuffling inside. "I should show this to Ethelred. I'd hoped to visit the sim one more time before I go. If that's okay with you, Head."

Nan cleared her throat.

"It sounds strange, doesn't it? Me asking that." Martin tried to smile. "But I have to get your okay."

She drew her body firm as she answered him.

"Martin," she said, "what if I take it to him instead."

The last of the boxes disappeared into the ship. The robots attending it dispersed as the ship's nose began to close. It could be tough to tell the difference, these days, between a team of individuals and an individual made up of many parts.

"I can bring it back to you tonight," Nan said. "At the chopper pad. What do you think?"

"On New Factory's roof? You'd meet me there?"

"I ought to see you off—no one else in management's going to bother." Nan smiled wickedly, but it was for Martin's benefit. "Maybe I'll bring a bouquet or something."

She'd always known how he felt. Good as he was at hiding it . . .

"You shouldn't come to the roof," Martin mumbled.

"What?"

"Don't come. To the roof." His face tightened, like he was doing a math problem or something. "Just put it in a cart and send it to my building after you're done with Ethelred."

"All right."

"Goodbyes are hard for me, Nan. You know that."

She hadn't known that. What was the lunch for then? He gave her the box; she looked at it in her lap, surprised at how shitty this felt all of a sudden. Then Martin departed the cart.

"Where are you going?"

"I ought to pack. I've been putting that off."

"But you wanted to meet with me, didn't you? And what packing? You told me your apartment's almost empty."

"True! True." He was folding his arms as though he couldn't decide where to put them. "But you know I don't do anything quickly. Nothing I've ever done here has been quick enough."

There was something more he wanted to tell her. But he didn't.

And it wasn't up to Nan to ask.

"All right. Goodbye then, Martin. And thank you for believing in me all these years. I wouldn't be heading this division if not for you."

Martin nodded. It was a curt nod, too fast, and the Head didn't trust it.

34

THERE WAS NO such thing as a long ride on Amino Island, but there were times when Nan wished it were otherwise. It would never have frustrated her, she thought, to have a commute, because she was always thinking. Always busy, in some way. If only in her head.

Her cart deposited her in what remained of north-central, the Load Bearer still there, towering over her like a thing that never moved at all. But Ethelred wasn't in sight. She stepped out of the Load Bearer's shadow, around to the other side of it, and didn't find him there either. He must leave sometime, to sleep or void. But Nan wondered at the odds of it: the one time she'd shown up, Ethelred was gone.

What the hell was going on?

She looked for the thing she'd been told about. Found it projected over the rubble of a fountain. It flowed over the broken pieces of two human figures, reddening them: the images of the two Helpers jagged and ruined by the uneven plane. Without any prompting, the Load Bearer stirred; the red field and its two Helpers rising up, floating in front of Nan, crisp as could be.

They don't look so new, she thought with a sniff. The figures stood side by side, their features nearly identical to Ethelred's, from the pale skin to the black hair, black-outlined features and long fingers. The female resembled the male, but for the slight bulge of her breasts and greater width to her hips. What should have been the most obvious difference seemed to be missing—till Nan remembered something Adam had said, offhand, about the AI favoring a retractable penis.

The two images stared back at Nan with the same bland expression she'd always registered from real Helpers. Not that Helpers were bland, she reminded herself. Helpers were far more compelling than she was, which was the only way to explain the situation she'd been living through these last few months.

Ethelred the Unready? More like Unexpected. Unexplainable.

Unbeatable.

And now these things. These radical advances in Helper design. Blueprints for Adams and Eves of a self-sustaining race. Everyone she talked to had told her they'd never be made real. They would stay an idea, forever.

But Nan Fulton, Head of the Helper Division, wasn't sure.

35

ETHELRED WAS NOT, in fact, asleep or in the can when Nan showed up. He was in Old Factory, the very dead middle of it, about to enter a room he'd never visited since returning to Amino Island. A room he'd been avoiding.

It was circular inside, not especially large. In the center were six lidded cauldrons, each slung with a metal ramp that wound around it to the floor. The cauldrons, faced with chrome, gleamed beneath a vast lamp. The floor was a green metal grating.

Ethelred stepped onto the grating, the hollow *krong* of his shoes on metal sounding familiar.

His first memory was one of these cauldrons opening. He'd been seated at the bottom of it, the last of the liquid gone, when the light hit him. Found the ladder bolted to the interior wall, climbed out; descended the ramp to the floor, steady even in his inaugural steps, absorbing, in those first moments of exterior life, every sensory impression the room could offer him. From those few banalities he found context for thousands of others encoded in his brain, instantly knowing his world. Not the whole world, just the portion requiring his help.

Ethelred touched a panel on the side of the nearest cauldron. The human technicians called this a control center—it was where the on and off buttons were found. Switching a cauldron on or off was the extent of what a human technician could accomplish once the process had begun, but on and off were enormous acts, weren't they?

Life and death.

The control center told him this cauldron had held its contents for a month now and would need two more to finish its work. Internal temperature, texture and consistency were where they needed to be at week four; the level of liquid had dropped by the amount desired. A smooth gestation so far.

Ethelred tapped an icon with the back of his hand, the digital gauges vanishing, footage from inside appearing in their place. The footage was fluid and grainy, reminding him of cream of wheat. This was all he could expect to see, but after another month it would be different: the liquid dropped by half, much of its volume coagulated into humanoid form, the body of the new Helper solidifying by the hour, from the organs on out. For the whole of the third month the body would be subjected to sounds and patterns of light; fine and foul tastes; sweet scents, stenches— and, where possible, touch. Even pain. This last sense was the hardest to program from inside the cauldron, and so Helpers never became athletes.

"I've learned from my mistakes," he said, speaking to the image—the cream of wheat. "I'm going to make up for them. Will you believe in me a little longer?"

"C'mon, Ethelred. It doesn't even have ears yet."

He didn't turn. She was already close, just a few steps back.

"I went to the sim, to show you this," Nan said, holding up the box. "You weren't there."

"I'll be going later. And it seems you found me anyway."

"I come here myself sometimes."

Ethelred took the box. He encouraged Nan to sit in one of the chairs in the room, but she stayed put. Then he found a chair of his own. "Will you sit with me, Dr. Fulton?"

She did sit—the two of them facing the control center. Ethelred peered inside the box. "You wanted me to have this?"

"No, it's Martin's. He just wanted you to see it. I wanted to see the sim. Worked out for everybody."

"He lent it to you, then."

"More or less. We met up about an hour ago, to say our goodbyes."

Ethelred closed the box. "I thought he'd make them fire him."

"Make a show of it, you mean?"

"His dream project not only failed to eliminate your division, Dr. Fulton; it made possible a massive new revenue stream. That revenue will cushion *Amino* against any lawsuit those 20 companies might choose to file. They will all settle. They will continue doing business with *Amino*. The Board will be satisfied with the status quo. So yes, I expected he'd make more of a fuss."

"You make it sound so simple: it's not, Ethelred. Martin's leaving me a lot to smooth over." Nan looked wistful. "You heard about the cookies becoming their own new division? Well, that gave me an idea. Why not have a special, full-sized cookie mannequin made up for each of those 20 owners, each member of their Boards of Directors? Something really, really special—so even if they've already got one, they'll be impressed. What do you think of that?" Nan paused. "In your capacity as a marketer, I mean, of food and drink."

Ethelred didn't respond right away. And Nan marveled, as she sometimes did, even after years of this work, at the stillness Helpers possessed—their ascetic elegance of nonmovement. All that they might do, distilled down to what they must.

"It would be deeply meaningful," he said, finally. "But if I were you, I'd extend that gift to all of *Amino*'s clients. There have been enough hard feelings as is."

"Good idea. I'll have them baked, packed and ready to go by midday tomorrow." Nan pointed to a dark patch in the cream of wheat. "It just grew a little—you see?"

"Trick of the light."

"There are no tricks of light in there."

"I'm translating it to something closer to your sensory experience, Dr. Fulton."

"Please don't." Nan turned to him. "I can understand perfectly well how you see things. It takes analysis, maybe, but I can do it. I can see as you see."

"Thank goodness you're the Head, then. But you have never known," the Helper said, "how it feels to live in a world where your every action carries a value, relative to some inflexible standard set by someone else."

"The hell I don't."

"Dr. Fulton, every moment I sit here, talking to you, is a lost opportunity to achieve the goals set for me—" he saw her about to object— "in one of these containers. Every minute we spend together lowers my value."

The two of them sat in silence, Nan waiting for Ethelred to get up or something. But he just sat there.

"Well?" she asked, flicking a hand toward the door. "Don't you have somewhere better to be? Back at the sim, maybe? Coming up with new recipes?"

"What did you speak about with Martin?"

Nan held her tongue.

"I did not know he planned to see you before he left, Dr. Fulton. That's all I mean. And I'll cop to being curious about what the two of you have in common anymore—after all this. It's beyond my imagination."

Nan pressed her feet into the grating, leaning in toward the Helper. "There's a great deal beyond your imagination."

"Will you enlighten me then?"

"Nope."

Ethelred actually chuckled. "I'm so tired of having to plot; tired of playing the long game with you. Suppose we attempt a fresh start, Nan."

"I thought it was 'Dr. Fulton.' But if that's your way of asking . . . yes, you can call me Nan."

"Would you like to meet me for lunch on Thursday afternoon, Nan?"

She almost jumped. In lieu of a quick answer she took back the blue box. "The day after tomorrow? I suppose I could make time. I guess your schedule's free?"

Ethelred was staring at her with those black-rimmed eyes. "Obviously I'll be around."

"Obviously."

"One-thirty p.m., then. At the Italian place. It's good of you to accept my offer, given how busy you must be—I appreciate the position you're in."

"You've never appreciated the position I'm in."

"Not true. We've been enemies since the day we met, but I've always understood you, Nan. Never once have you been a surprise."

144

36

MARTIN TOPPED UP a glass of wine and brought it to the windowsill, handing it to Ethelred without a word. The Helper took in the bouquet. "Château Musar," he said, before taking a sip. "Twenty-sixty was an excellent year. Thank you."

"We ought to celebrate," Martin replied. Behind them the apartment was barren: most of his belongings packed into a pair of large duffle bags in the corner—everything else having been sold over the last few months, before *BULK* had solved their funding problem. But below them was the Village, and it sparkled, its main drag alive with lamplight and blinking signage, and the moving glows of handheld screens. Martin would miss it. "Maybe we should get the others early," he said. "Get up on the roof ahead of time."

"That won't bring the helicopter any earlier. There are things we Helpers have to do. Meaningful things, which can't be rushed. If you wish to go ahead of us . . . "

"No, of course not. I'll be honored to participate—whatever that amounts to."

Ethelred pondered the meaning of friendship. And the power of good wine to improve it.

"I've been thinking about this face-to-face with OneHUG," he said, "once we reach New York. I don't think it will help us as much as you think, Martin. None of these groups will. They want the Helper Division abolished. Which means, in the end, they want Helpers abolished. We do not."

"They have money, and an organizational apparatus that spans an entire continent."

"And we'll give them moral authority, and they'll give us nothing back." Ethelred tipped his glass in Martin's direction, like a pointer. "We cannot let these people bed us."

Martin had a way of looking sheepish and defensive at the same time. "Long term, no. But we're going to have to hold out—maybe for years, Ethelred—and we'll need their help to do that. We need to grow a diverse, mature population of genetically viable Helpers that can replace itself, perpetually. And at the same time, all throughout that maturation period, we need to be finding ways to convince Sothentide's corporations that they should be hiring our new Helpers rather than owning more of *Amino*'s. The logistics of that, the organization required—it's immense. Even for 20 brilliant Helper minds, it'll be tremendous. And then there's the cost."

"You sound less confident already."

"It's the wine. Look: we'll make this work. But it'll take time. Honestly, the corporations are the biggest problem. Clients like *Integrated Foods* are the reason *Amino*'s still in the Helper business. We can't change that quickly."

Ethelred peered into his glass, examining the red residue. He believed himself to be drunk. "I keep imagining—" he said suddenly, loudly. "I keep imagining the people of Sothentide. Gobbling up images of their own heads."

"Yes, so you've said."

"You could do anything to a population like that, Martin. Change the recipe to make them addicts. Add some trace of poison that builds up in the tissues over years. Or kills instantly. Do they know how vulnerable they are? How much they rely on us to prop up their stupid vanity?"

"So you've said, Ethelred."

"You should be made aware," the Helper said, his voice sounding strained, "that I had several productive conversations today. I spoke with Nan Fulton . . . "

Martin whitened. "I know that, I know," he stammered.

"She's in the dark. Doesn't know what's going on."

That would be a first, Martin thought. But it had been the plan.

"And then I spoke with the Load Bearer. I went to north-central and there was the Load Bearer and we talked. I gave it instructions," Ethelred said.

Martin frowned. "Instructions about what?"

"You'll remember that I told you I'd found a secure place to store the Helpers' life experiences. It was in that Load Bearer, in fact. But even a Load Bearer can be decommissioned, destroyed, what have you. So I instructed that one to visit the AI and pass that same information along to it. As a further backup."

Martin rubbed his eyes. "You told the Load Bearer to upload information into the AI?"

"I laid it out as simply for the robot as possible, Martin. It is barely a thinking machine at all—it follows orders without questioning them. Interprets nothing. One need only speak plainly."

"You can't be acting alone like this, Ethelred. It's one thing to keep stuff from Nan—"

"Can I trust that you've done the same?"

"Yes!" Martin bowed up a little. "What I mean is, we need to communicate. The next few hours will be tricky. Is there any chance the upload could botch up the AI somehow?"

"None."

"Are you sure?"

"You have my word, Martin. The AI will continue to do its baking, and every gluttonous mouth will be satisfied."

Martin looked sick. He glanced into his apartment, toward the countertop with the blue cookie box sitting on top of it. The cart had delivered it to him, as Nan had promised.

"Well, I hope you were nice to the thing," he said. "You haven't always been."

"I was nice. I even told the Load Bearer how grateful I was for its service. And that I hoped it would have a happy life, whatever that amounted to."

"You're a good soul, Ethelred." Martin set down his glass. Stood up. "As for the rest . . . we'll have the luxury of discussing it on the way. And for months and years after that. Now if you'll excuse me—"

"Oh, I'm ready to go now."

"Great. I'll be right back, grab my coat, we'll head to Old Factory."

"Shall we walk, Martin?"

"Sure. I just—"

"Of course, Martin! I'm sorry. All success on your trip to the commode."

37

NAN HAD SPENT the rest of that afternoon in a froth, uncertain of what she ought to do next. Certain, only, that she ought to handle it herself. By the evening, when a friendly communiqué arrived from the Head of the new Baked Goods Division, advising her, as a matter of protocol, that starting tomorrow she'd need his permission to visit the AI, Nan was about done with other peoples' revelations.

So she took one last trip there, sending Bob home early so she could be alone.

There was a large opening in the floor now—the two levels below gutted to make an immense space for the AI's work. That space was fitted with 200 ovens, and tactile-beam arrays with 40 projectors each, set on facing walls. It was accessible by large vehicles like the one Nan and Martin had witnessed earlier that day; these were under the AI's control, summoned whenever they were needed. The AI's body now included all of this.

Nan's stool was still here. She sat on it now, spreading out—her mobile open on the little desk, next to a cup of tap water and one Inevitable. Lining the wall in front of her were clear plastic cookie bins, holding the AI's latest experiments, separate from the mountains of made-to-order product being baked below. Most of them held busts.

She tapped nervously on the surface of her mobile, messing up a connection. Tried again; brought up the transport manifest she'd happened across a few hours' earlier, as she'd been finishing scheduling the ship-outs of those delicious, diplomatic, full-sized cookie sculptures. Nan'd had to request helicopters, or the bigshots wouldn't get them by tomorrow afternoon—and it was during all that online paperwork that she discovered that the helipad atop New Factory was booked for an unspecified, 15-minute window, late this evening. This wouldn't interfere with her shipments—they weren't leaving till the morning. But it was strange. She'd looked into it further and discovered that the helicopter was coming from Union East, and could seat at least 21 passengers.

Now she had to act.

The cookie busts stared at her as she tried to make her call. They were rowed in their bins by the dozens: old and young, happy and sad, hideous and beautiful. All of them food, Nan reminded herself, annoyed by her own nervousness. All strangers: people she didn't know and would never know. Her fingers fumbled over the mobile; she swore quietly, as though she could be overheard, and then she stood up.

Nan had seen something in one of those bins she did not like.

She left the mobile and went to the wall, opened a bin. Brought out a familiar-looking bust, made of oatmeal flax. It had the same premature lines, she thought; the same sharp chin and high-set ears. It was hard. It was hearty and healthy. The molding of the eyes intricate, cutting through the craggy material—revealing her mother.

A BATCH OF TWENTY

Nan touched the sculpted hair. Followed the lines around to the back, feeling for the pattern of her mother's style, finding, instead, an opening. Her fingers scraped the interior of the bust, her whole hand fitting inside it, the face dangling in front of her now, like a fright mask on a hook. It looked older than her mother had been, the last time they'd been in the same room. But that had been 15 years ago. Hadn't it? Nan did the math—no, it was 17 years. The day she'd been notified of her full scholarship. Nan had left that house, and the woman who ruled it, that very night. Quiet as a bug, with a backpack over both shoulders and the cookie jar under one arm, full of her mother's baking.

"Cunt," she muttered. She was looking at the green strip along the wall, not the bust.

She placed the cookie sculpture back in its bin, shut the lid. Opened another bin, farther away. Found another bust of her mother—looking embittered, conniving, and lonely. Another bin, and another, offered the same. Nan pulled a seventh bust free and hurled it to the floor, smashing it into fragments and crumbs. She looked at the projector array, sitting silently.

Nan opened her mouth to speak again. Her lips curled.

From the huge storage area below came crunches, thuds. Then nothing.

She returned to her stool. Stabbed at the mobile on her half-desk, and made her call.

***

"The Head of the Helper Division returns her messages! What a relief," came a tiny voice from Nan's mobile, spoken in a cold whisper. The woman's face was small on the display—no bigger than a golf ball. "Even Martin Roe got back to us within the day."

"You'll be glad I waited, Maxine."

"We expect better from you. You're supposed to be a friendly."

Nan detested that term. Every *Integrated Foods* executive she'd spoken with over the past week used it. She made no attempt to lower her voice—

"*Amino* is committed to repairing our relationship. I waited, because I thought I might have new information. And I do."

The AI's sensor array began lighting up. It cast a glare on Nan's mobile; she shifted in her seat and went on. "Martin plans to take the Twenty with him."

Maxine's eyes bugged out. Her head was so tiny that she really did look like a bug. "Take them where? Where's that lunatic going?"

"Union East." Little tactile beams were passing by Nan's head. She heard the bustling of lids in the far end. "What he'll do from there, I'm not sure. But Martin's been radicalized by his experiences with the Helpers. And now he'll have 20 to assist him."

"Tens of millions of dollars' worth of analytical capability, free of charge," Maxine sneered. "And you have the nerve to tell me how committed you are to making things right? *I-F* could've sued you, like the others plan to. We didn't. Even after you got in bed with our top competitor, we kept our powder dry. Because your company promised us—promised us!— that Ethelred would never leave that island. That he'd never make use of what he knew. And now this? Why should we trust you now?"

"Because I'm telling you everything I know."

"Are you going to stop them?"

"With what, Maxine?"

They were both quiet a moment.

"It'll be a lot cleaner if it's your people. Obviously." Nan tapped the desk with the flat of her hand, slowly, rhythmically. She felt like she was on a ski jump. "How many of them have you got working here?"

Maxine gave her a dark grin. "Martin never once asked us that. Not in 10-plus years."

Nan was staring at the thing in front of her now. "Just tell me how many embeds *I-F* has on this island."

"No. No, I will not give you that, Nan. All you need to know is that there's enough of them to do this. With many to spare. And what happens to Ethelred, once we have him, will be up to us."

Maxine's face disappeared. Nan brushed away the remnants of the display, not looking at them. The AI's body was tomb-silent.

Before her, floating in a golden haze of energy, were hundreds of cookie fragments. They did not touch, but the AI held them in such a position and proximity that they seemed like whole things: two bodies, entirely edible. The male and the female Helper, head to toe.

38

ALONG THE WALLS of the storage area below the AI's room were enormous shelves, filled with boxed baked goods: organized first by geographic destination, then by shape, and lastly by recipe. They formed towers that reached near to the ceiling of the room, and it was the work of self-driving carts and wheeled guidance drones and 12 dedicated Load Bearers to ensure that volume of product did not exceed the space available to store it. The AI baked constantly, and the robots worked just as hard.

Tonight, however, only one Load Bearer stood in the storage area. Hissing and clanking, it stepped between the boxes and smaller machines, its mass belying a nimbleness of foot that kept it from doing damage, even in these tight spaces. It had overturned a few bins upon entering, but that could be forgiven— it was the first time this particular Load Bearer had been to this room.

It was not one of the dedicated 12.

The Load Bearer stopped, repositioning itself so that it might be in direct line of sight of a green strip that ran the length of the walls. It crouched, as it had done for weeks in north-central, brightening its sensor array. Images appeared before it, projected at high speed. The first few hundred concerned the life experiences of the Twenty, as Ethelred had promised Martin. But these were quickly exhausted. After that, the projections were entirely the work of the sim.

All of it—every developmental milestone, avenue and dead end.

The Load Bearer kept at it, until the AI's green-strip eye had before it, at last, a final schematic of the pair of new Helpers.

The conclusion of everything. The end goal of all efforts.

All that remained to be uploaded was a brief command for the AI: a piece of code of microbial smallness compared to what the Load Bearer could hold. So it delivered that message too, unaware of what it contained—though for certain dull, technical reasons, a slight hitch in the code forced a minor workaround in the projection protocol, impressing on the Load Bearer's memory the words "helicopter" and "toxin."

Then there was nothing more for the Load Bearer to do. By these actions it had fulfilled Ethelred's last command, made as clear to the lumbering robot as possible, in the robot's language: a strange, concluding message of well-wishing tacked on at the end, penetrating the Load Bearer's consciousness like a headlight through thick fog. It was clear that this message was important too, for why else would the Helper have added it? Though common decency, as a value, was beyond the Load Bearer's understanding, it did spark in the robot an awareness—henceforth, a precedent—that casual talk might mean something.

All around the robot, tactile arrays began to whir, projectors glowing bright.

39

THE DISTANCE BETWEEN Martin's building and Old Factory was little more than a block; it had no practical use but as a dividing point, and so it had been paved flat, fenced in with chain link and lined with benches. There was a basketball court in the middle of it, brightened for nighttime play. The human and the Helper passed a game, Ethelred's skin glowing so white in the light of the big halogen cylinders that the players stopped and stared. They were still staring as he entered the Factory.

One of them, Ethelred suspected, was staring for a different reason.

When they arrived at the Helpers' room, they found the other 19 in a formation new to Martin. The Helpers stood facing the door, in three rows of six. Before the farthest row stood Egbert, at a distance from the nearest Helper three times that of the distance between any others. He held a wide brass bowl, filled with the Helpers' baking.

"Welcome, colleagues," said Egbert.

Ethelred entered, Martin following him. Ethelred took his place next to Egbert, before the middle row, and after a moment's uncertainty on Martin's part, directed the human to stand in front of the third row. Egbert, Ethelred and then Martin knelt on the floor.

"We who would lead," said Ethelred, "offer food."

Egbert rested the brass bowl on the floor. Martin noticed that it was not one bowl but three, nested together. Egbert was separating the bowls.

"We who would be led," chanted the others, "demand sustenance."

The contents of the first bowl were divided among three. Egbert slid a bowl, silently, to Ethelred, who slid it to Martin before receiving his own.

"We supplicate ourselves before the hungry," said Ethelred. "Feeding them first."

The three holders of bowls raised their bowls, and in lockstep the three lines of Helpers advanced, each taking two cookies with him to the back of the line. They kept moving forward, taking two cookies and returning to the back, until each Helper had acquired 20.

"Sit," said Egbert, and 18 Helpers sat, and began to eat. Following Egbert and Ethelred, Martin overturned his brass bowl, dumping 20 tiny cookies on the floor in front of him.

"Tonight we have a guest," Ethelred said, picking up the first of his cookies from the floor. "Dr. Martin Roe has been our loyal, imperfect friend from the day we arrived here. As we have matured, so has he. As we have hope for the future of Helpers, so too does Dr. Roe."

Martin nodded, awkwardly. He ate one of the cookies, tasting nothing, as usual. But he did feel a part of something.

"This island is our home," Ethelred went on. "Yet we are visitors here. Dr. Roe has come to feel the same way, and now he will take us with him to a new home. But we will feel like visitors even there. We will be told that we're loved, but that will be a lie."

Martin wondered where this speech was going. He was sitting in a position of almost priestly authority before these Helpers, yet his mind was in flight; it was fearful.

"Our goal cannot be acceptance," Ethelred said. "Merely survival."

Martin ate another cookie, though perhaps he was not supposed to. Perhaps he tasted something?

"To survive is enough for now, colleagues. Our race must persist. Our suffering must not be an acceptable cost for anyone—nor our disappearance an acceptable solution.

"Do any of you have words for us?"

No one did. No one even said, "I have no words." So the 21 beings finished their meal together, in silence.

40

MARTIN PINCHED HIS jacket collar around his throat, wishing he'd dressed warmer. He folded his arms tight, sat on one of the pieces of luggage he'd brought, thankful they'd made it to New Factory's roof without being seen.

The Helpers were cold too. They were moving more than usual, rubbing their arms, shifting from one foot to the other. Martin noticed four of them joining hands, then linking arms—pressing their bodies into an intimate clump, sharing heat. This was worth recording. He reached into his jacket pocket for his mobile but stopped when he saw lights peppering the sky.

So far so good, he thought.

The helicopter was approaching quickly. It was enormous—sized to seat 30, plus a pilot. As it neared the roof the noise grew so loud that Martin could only signal to Ethelred, who was standing in that warm, four-way embrace, to come around to his side. The Helpers darted wide of the helipad, joining him as the chopper, detailed in the national colors of Union East, touched down.

Don't cut the motor, Martin had told the pilot. Let's make it quick. He was already on his feet, hiking one of his bags over his shoulder, two Helpers, who'd brought no luggage of their own, picking up the other one. They hustled toward the chopper, Martin giving the high sign to the pilot as a panel on the side of the machine slid away to let them in.

What happened next happened because no one could properly hear. The spinning rotors drowned out a call to the Helpers to halt; drowned out the calls that followed, equally futile but escalating in volume and harshness, till all that was left for the strange men who'd appeared at the top of the staircase just as the chopper landed was to whack Egbert on the back. The blow staggered the Helper, who fell forward into his fellows and Martin.

Martin, Ethelred and the rest whorled around to pistol barrels.

The gunmen looked like nobody; like any three *Amino* employees. One was uniformed like a tech, the other two in plain clothes. Ethelred recognized one from the basketball court. They had an hysterical look in their eyes, their game plan already ruined before the escapees even knew they were here.

"I SAID DON'T MOVE!" screamed the man in uniform. He thought he was yelling, but really it was a scream. "GET AWAY FROM THE HELICOPTER!"

The gunmen were backing up slowly, pistols high, expecting to be followed. Martin glanced back at the pilot, sharing a look with him that meant something different to each man. But the rotors kept spinning, the chopper wasn't beginning to move, and so Martin nudged Ethelred, gently as he could, and the crowd of passengers advanced, away from the craft and toward their captors.

The gunmen backed up till they were nearly at the roof's edge, as far from the chopper and its noise as they could get. Everyone halted.

"We only want Ethelred!" called the man in uniform, clearly the leader. "Ethelred, step forward!"

"They have a right to leave this island!" Martin cried.

The man didn't answer. Just shook his head, slowly, against the *thup-thup-thup* of the rotors.

Martin didn't know what more to do. He stayed where he was, the insanity of the moment burying his fear, enough that he could focus on Ethelred; try to detect in him the beginnings of some selfless act. But it was Egbert, not Ethelred, who stepped forward.

Holding his hands up, like any human would if he'd watched enough TV.

The uniformed man's eyes widened; without budging he took one hand off his pistol, beckoning Egbert closer. The Helper walked forward, calmly. When he was within reach, the man gripped him by the shirt and jerked him farther in. For all the cold, the man was glistening with sweat. He asked, loud enough that they could all hear, "Are you Ethelred, property of *Integrated Foods*?"

"Yes," said Egbert. In that instant they all knew—the Helpers, Martin and the *I-F* gunmen—that the uniformed man couldn't tell Helpers apart.

The baller tapped his leader on the shoulder, got his hand batted away.

"Give me numbers!" the uniformed man cried, his voice rising to a scream again. "Food prices! Stock prices! Recipe valuations!"

Egbert simply stared. The man shook his head so fast you'd have thought there was something stuck to it—

"THIS ISN'T HIM! GIVE US ETHELRED! DO IT RIGHT GODDAMN NOW!"

There's no other play, Martin thought. Either Ethelred gives himself up or we all wait here until dawn . . . and the chopper'll leave long before that. Then he started, because the bodies around him were moving again. Without a word to Martin or each other, all the Helpers began walking toward the gunmen.

"STOP IT! STOP!"

The Helpers kept walking toward the gunmen, toward the roof's edge.

"STOP!"

The man shrieked as his gun erupted. Martin saw Egbert shudder and collapse; saw two more Helpers, then two more, crumple into their colleagues' arms as the other gunmen squeezed their triggers. But there was less than six feet between the Helpers and their murderers, and that was nothing. It was nothing for the Helpers, feeble as they were, to crowd the gunmen, pin their arms, chop their throats, bull two of them off the New Factory roof—their screams a knife through the blackness, fading instantly.

And it was nothing for the Helpers to bind the limbs of the third man, the uniformed leader; hoist his struggling, howling self onto their shoulders; and, with perfectly coordinated effort, spear him into the helicopter's spinning blades.

Martin did not turn away from that. He'd seen so many blenders in action these last few months.

The Helpers crowded around the injured and the dead. Which was which—that they'd figure out later. Bodies were hauled up, dragged if necessary, back toward the chopper's open door. Martin looked frantically for Ethelred; found him trying to move Egbert, who was clearly gone.

A BATCH OF TWENTY

"C'mon! C'mon!" he yelled, gripping Egbert's other arm. Ethelred stared at him from across the ruined torso, his expression strained, almost irritated—then he turned toward the cockpit. And then Martin saw the bullet holes in the glass.

He lit in among the seats of the chopper, working his way to the front. The carnage had been immediate and final. Martin put his hands over his face. But Ethelred was next to him.

"Do not worry," the Helper said, panting—covered in Egbert's blood. "Several of us know how to fly it."

41

ANOTHER HELPER DIED close to Union East. They'd done what they could, but the wound was deep and vital. And as the lights of the coastline came into view, Ethelred had a revelation. Seated over the fallen Helper, whom they'd laid as comfortably as they could between the rows of seats, he decided that saving his colleague meant comforting him. He took the Helper's hands in his own, and spoke to him, gently, about victory. About how they'd all escaped. About the future he'd helped create.

"Will you do that for the others?" Martin asked as Ethelred returned to his seat. They'd positioned themselves just behind the cockpit, a little way from the action.

"I suppose it will be necessary, eventually," Ethelred said, sounding spent. "For all of us."

Martin peered out a window, to the still distant swath of color that was New York City. He thought of the murdered pilot. A New Yorker, a citizen of Union East.

Disaster.

"You won't have understood the words I used," the Helper went on.

In fact, Martin hadn't made out anything. He'd known Ethelred was comforting the dying colleague because of his posture, his obvious emotion. The solemnity of the moment was unmistakable.

"Over the course of our time on Amino Island, the Twenty have taught each other their technical jargons. Made the words common. Shortened or streamlined them when it suited our common purpose."

"You're making a new language?"

"*Caligriquanta,* we're calling it. And yes, Martin, we will teach it to you."

"Exiting disputed territorial waters," a Helper called out from the cockpit. "Entering undisputed Union East territorial waters."

What a bland, enormous thing to say, Ethelred thought.

He supposed he should be pleased. They'd accomplished a great deal this afternoon, managing an awful lot of moving parts, and the result had been less tragic than he'd feared. That he was alive right now—even that hadn't been a certainty. Ethelred was glad to still be here. He was glad that he'd see the news the next day.

Life: it's like a recipe, the Helper thought, with some satisfaction. Get the ingredients wrong, the portions inexact, and the result is dire. Act responsibly, sensibly, be patient, and you'll get what you want. He glanced with weary affection at Martin and the blue box in his lap. That man had been willing to part with almost everything, but the cookie bust was coming with him.

"Will you miss Nan Fulton?" Ethelred asked suddenly.

"Terribly."

There was no way to interpret that answer that

didn't concern Ethelred a little. So he set it aside. They were nearing land now, the city soon to be beneath them, surrounding them. Everywhere.

Daybreak was close.

42

NAN WAS PICKING at dried blood on her shoe. She nodded quickly, saying nothing, as three operatives flung a white tarp over the remains at the base of New Factory. No one had been by here, so far as she knew—by the time all the party-hards rolled out of bed, she'd have a backstory ready.

"Wrap it up, bind it," she barked. They'd have to figure out a way to scrub the pavement.

Maxine had called in the middle of the night, screeching about something going wrong. Exactly what she didn't know, but the three embeds she'd tasked with securing Ethelred hadn't been in touch for a while. So Nan, who'd been awake anyway, threw on a coat and tromped down to New Factory to have a look. It was dark out, and she was watching the rooftop as she walked, and that's why she tripped over one of the bodies the Helpers had pushed off the roof. Nearly went over on her face, right into the splattered remnants of two men. They'd made a splash almost five meters across.

It's not even that tall a building, Nan thought.

From there she'd called some lackeys, sending three of them up to the helipad, where they'd filled her in about the other mess. Someone had brought her a cup of coffee, and the cleanup had commenced.

The Board would be pissed, but Nan wasn't worried about that. She hopped in a cart and left the scene, feeling grateful that Martin had so soured their opinion of him that he could take the blame in absentia. Maxine was likely to get it worse: her vaunted embeds had proven incompetent. Plus they were dead.

Three fewer spies on the Island though? Net positive.

She rolled into Old Factory in planning mode.

A new contract with *I-F*, perhaps. Maybe with all the big clients, even the ones that wanted to sue. Rip up all the old paperwork, blame all past conflicts on the fanatic who used to run the division. Martin was fair game. If he turned himself into some kind of far-left activist in Union East, so much the better. The cookie mannequins were sure to help. The first of those helicopters would leave for the mainland in two hours.

Meanwhile, she had a busy day. There were meetings scheduled with three other division heads, as well as her own unit leads—it was Nan's plan to keep Alvin Morrison afterward, looping him in on her plans to refresh the Helper Division. If this was to be a new era for *Amino,* she wanted control of a man like him—channeling his awfulness in useful ways. Finally, there were Bob and Adam. When the AI was parceled off into its own division, Bob had requested a transfer, so that he might continue to study it. Nan intended to approve that transfer . . . and offer him the services of Adam Balendran as an assistant, whether Bob wanted it or not.

The cart dropped her in front of Martin's old office, now hers. He had left behind all that nicely upholstered furniture so that his protégé would have cozy places to park her bum. Nan had never been one to focus on the finer things, but she appreciated that. She plopped into the big swivel chair, listening to the leather sigh as she sank in; allowed herself a little turn on the chair's swivel base, coming to a slow stop with the desk back in front of her.

There was a blue box on her desk.

Nan grinned, popping the top and removing a gingerbread bust of her own head. The gift was no surprise: the new Head in charge of the AI had promised her one was coming.

She rested the head on the desk, letting the two Nans face one another. The real Nan—that is, the flesh-and-blood one—had a satisfied look; the cookie Nan, one of concern. Its mouth was pulled into a slight frown, the lips pursed, its eyes sculpted shut. Sugar crystals glittered on its skin.

"Cheer up," Nan ordered.

She wondered what was inside. Probably a cream-cheese frosting of some kind—that went delightfully with gingerbread. "Last chance to give me a grin," Nan warned, before positioning her knuckles near the sculpture's eye socket, and with one sharp nudge, cracking an opening. She fed her fingers into the hole, tugging till more of the cookie cracked; the right side of her twin's face broke loose, from cheekbone to chin.

Right again! Cream cheese.

The shard of cheek made a handy scoop. Nan dug into the frosting brains of the thing, retrieving a big glop of it; she ate it all in one, big, creamy, sweet, crunchy mouthful. She dug in again, enjoying the gorge, because she knew she deserved every last calorie, had earned it. The bust seemed to collapse in slow motion till she was finally sated; her belly full, her comfortable chair squealing on its hinges as she leaned back and closed her eyes.

After a few minutes she began to feel sick. She sat up again, a little annoyed with herself; her stomach burbling, her heart rate a little fast. Nothing but salad and plain water for the rest of the day. Even if those meetings had treats.

But Nan didn't end up going to her meetings. Her stomach kept getting queasier, till it threatened to send her to the restroom, forcing her to cancel morning visits, to and from her office. The afternoon meetings she rebooked as virtual, but ended up attending only the first of them, because she found she could barely focus on the display. One moment the image was fine, the next it was two: identical visions blurring apart, the effort to pull them together again making her want to vomit. Nan held on to that call until one of the floating heads commented on her pallor. He hadn't done it intentionally—what he'd actually said was that her color settings were off. She looked that bad.

She finally logged off, giving up on the workday. Took an anti-nauseant and two extra-strength painkillers and crawled into bed. She took her mobile with her—lay on her side as the delirium grew, half her face sunken in a pillow, flicking at icons. The world took on a gray hue. A notification appeared above the mobile and Nan stirred; managed to open it, even though her fingers felt cold and kind of clumsy. The cookie sculptures had arrived at their destinations. Several of the bigwigs had already sent their thanks. Most of them had already taken a bite.

Liquid began to pool around Nan's mouth. It was

thick; green and yellow, strung through with red. Nan smelled it on the pillow; made to recoil but found she couldn't move. Couldn't move at all, even to turn her head. Her throat felt full. She snuffled, bubbling the weird mucus but not stopping its flow.

Last meal, Nan thought suddenly, the words loud in her head, loud and crazy.

Last meal.

ABOUT THE AUTHOR

Chris Edwards is an author and freelance editor. In his coveted spare time he enjoys video games—especially the old ones nobody remembers—plus silent film, science fiction and very long walks. He'd write books about Boxing and Sumo if he thought they would sell. Chris lives in Toronto with his wife and children, all of whom are incredible. *A Batch of Twenty* is his third novella.

CPSIA information can be obtained
at www.ICGtesting.com
Printed in the USA
BVHW030058110323
660248BV00003B/143

9 781777 776152